"This will just take a minute," she said, kneeling in front of me. She had a row of pins between her lips and her words were garbled. Now and then, the backs of her hands brushed against my thighs as she worked, sending disturbing signals up my body. I was glad she was focused on the hemming job, because my nipples had grown quite erect again. I couldn't believe the way my damn body was responding to something as innocent as having someone hem a dress.

But it wasn't just that, I knew. For one thing, I found Dr. Lauren Monroe damned attractive, and for another thing, the dress I was wearing made me feel totally exposed. She was only inches away, touching me, and I could feel her breath on my thighs. It had been a long, long time. I drew in a lengthy sigh and let it out slowly, trying not to shudder.

"There," she said, patting my hip as she got to her feet. "That wasn't so bad, was it?" Obviously, she had no idea.

She stood back and examined her work, and I saw her take in the condition of my nipples. Her eyes met mine and there was an instant of absolute, irrefutable recognition.

LOOKING FOR NAIAD?

Buy our books at
www.naiadpress.com

or call our toll-free number
1-800-533-1973

or by fax (24 hours a day)
1-850-539-9731

5th Wheel

A CASSIDY JAMES MYSTERY

BY

KATE CALLOWAY

THE NAIAD PRESS, INC.
1998

Printed in the United States of America on acid-free paper
First Edition

Editor: Christine Cassidy
Cover designer: Bonnie Liss (Phoenix Graphics)
Typesetter: Sandi Stancil

Library of Congress Cataloging-in-Publication Data

Calloway, Kate, 1957 –
    Fifth wheel : a Cassidy James mystery / by Kate Calloway.
        p.   cm.
    Fifth installment in the mystery series featuring Cassidy James.
    ISBN 1-56280-218-6   (alk. paper)
    I. Title.
PS3553.A4245F59   1998
813'.54—dc21   98-13220
                                                                    CIP

For my mother,
who teaches me daily
what it means to be a strong woman.

Acknowledgments

A heartfelt thanks to my friends (again!) for taking the time to read and critique a work in progress. You are all so brave and kind. Special thanks to my unofficial eiditor, Carol, who keeps me honest, and to Christi Cassidy, my other editor, for her encouragement and unerring eye. As always, thanks to my friends and family for their continued support and to those readers who have offered such kind feedback.

About the Author

Kate Calloway was born in 1957. She has published several novels with Naiad including *First Impressions, Second Fiddle, Third Degre,* and *Fourth Down,* all in the Cassidy James Mystery Series. Her short stories appear in *Lady Be Good* and *Dancing in the Dark.* Her hobbies include cooking, wine-tasting, boating, song-writing and spending time with Carol. They split their time between southern California and the Pacific Northwest; the latter is the setting for the Cassidy James novels. Those who know Kate well say that Cassidy James is not entirely fictional.

Chapter One

He watched his next victim step off the bus and felt the excitement surge through him like a warm electric current. It pricked his skin with a pleasant burning sensation and he trembled, confident he'd chosen well.

He anticipated her fear and swallowed hard. He was an empathetic guy, after all. When they begged for mercy, his own throat always tightened with emotion. When they pleaded, quite often his own eyes welled up with tears. So it wasn't unusual for him to feel their fear, even before they felt it themselves. Like now, he thought, watching her move with the carefree confidence of someone who didn't realize her time was almost up.

Dressed in a tight black skirt and pale pink silk blouse, she was oblivious to his presence. That would change, though. It always did. Just thinking about that special moment, when she'd get that first inkling of his existence, made him sweat with longing. That was always the best part, that first undefined fear, when they sensed him, looked over their shoulder, and unconsciously quickened their pace.

But for now, he practiced nonchalance. There was plenty of time.

He licked his lips and sauntered forward. She was leaning over, one foot on the bus-stop bench, replacing the black heels she'd worn to work with a pair of Nike tennis shoes for the walk home. He'd seen her do this before, had known she'd do it today.

"Excuse me," he said, stepping back to avoid the collision as she moved to put her other foot on the bench. His nostrils flared, taking in the heady scent of her perfume.

"Hey," she said, glaring at him for an instant, before her face softened. It was the same look he'd seen her use on the grocery store clerk last week, a mixture of impatience and annoyance. She recovered her manners in time to say, "I didn't know you were there. Sorry."

He'd barely brushed against her, but the contact was almost more than he could bear. He wanted to take her right then and there, and he felt the knife inside his pants, cool metal against his burning skin, calling to him. It took tremendous control to ignore it. But control was his specialty.

"No problem," he managed. For one brief second he let his eyes meet hers. There was no fear in them, which excited him even more. Because he knew that soon there would be. And it would be because of him.

Chapter Two

"Nobody barbecues in the rain," Rick said, sticking his head out the sliding glass door. He set four beers on the deck and disappeared back into the warmth of the house. Sheriff Booker went to retrieve them.

"He's got a point," he said, handing Towne a bottle of Red Dog Ale.

We were standing around the Weber under the overhang, warming our hands over the black kettle. The turkey inside was sizzling and the aroma was incredible. My best friend, Martha Harper, slipped her arm around my shoulders and pulled me close.

"You cold?"

I shook my head, trying not to shiver. "I'm hungry," I said.

"So what else is new?" the three of them chimed in unison. I laughed. No point in denying it. I was a self-avowed glutton. Luckily, I had a fast metabolism.

The rain was coming down in a steady torrent and Rainbow Lake was riddled with dimples. There was no breeze at all, but the late November air was chilly. I was tempted to join the others in the kitchen, but I was fascinated with the case Booker and Martha were discussing.

"The FBI done a profile on the guy yet?" Booker asked. His blue eyes looked almost gray, matching the slate-colored clouds. His silver moustache twitched, as it always did when he was thinking. Approaching sixty, Sheriff Booker was still as handsome as ever.

"Hell, Tom, they're just now getting around to admitting that it might be a serial killer. I guess one woman wasn't enough. Now that we found a second body down in Gold Beach, they finally sent out a couple of rookies. One of them looks about sixteen. I'm not kidding. He's got zits and everything." Martha laughed, but her big brown eyes looked worried. "Anyway, they ran the stats through VICAP, but so far nothing's turned up, so it looks like this guy is just starting out."

Ever since she'd found the first victim six months ago, brutally murdered and dumped along Highway 101, Martha's eyes had been puffed with the tell-tale signs of insomnia. I'd never seen her so consumed with a case, and even Tina, Martha's longest-lasting Significant Other to date, seemed unable to quell Martha's anxiety.

I knew that the first victim, Sarah Ringer, had been a student at Kings Harbor Community College. Her mutilated body had been found propped against a fifty-year-old cedar by a passing motorist on the highway. She'd been bound, beaten, chewed on, cut up and raped. The cause of death had been strangulation, though the other wounds would likely have killed her eventually. Weirder still, the M.E. had found a semen-filled condom inside her vagina, which the general public did not know. It had been tied on one end like a balloon, trapping its contents inside. Even before the second victim, Tracy Lee, was found, Martha had worried that she might be seeing the work of a serial killer. She'd tried to get Captain Grimes to enlist the help of the FBI then, but he wasn't interested.

"Why do you think it might be a serial killer?" I'd asked her one night. We'd been drinking red wine with our dinner and had taken the rest of the bottle out to the hot tub.

"Because one thing serial killers have in common, Cass, is that they tend to take souvenirs. Sarah Ringer was missing her pinky finger." This was another detail the general public was not privy to.

The second victim, Tracy Lee, also a young woman, had lived in Gold Beach, about a hundred miles south of Kings Harbor. She was a clerk in a video store, had never been to college and, aside from being young and attractive, didn't seem to have much in common with Sarah Ringer. Martha had explained that many serial killers go after the same type, but Sarah's blond hair and blue eyes contrasted sharply with the Asian woman's darker features. What the two victims did have in common was the horrific way in which their bodies had been mutilated prior to death, and the way the killer had positioned them along the side of the road.

"Look at that," Martha had said, showing me two grisly crime scene photos. "He's displaying them like works of art. He props them up, and see their hands?"

"Looks like they're praying," I said, trying to quell a surge of nausea. Both women had been propped against trees, their legs crossed at the ankles, heads bowed, hands clasped in their laps.

"Or maybe he's covering their genitals. The bastard's definitely trying to send a message of some kind."

If anything, the second murder had been more brutal than the first. Tracy Lee had been bound, beaten, bitten, stabbed, sliced and finally choked to death. The big toe on her left foot was missing, and like Sarah, she'd had a semen-filled condom inserted into her vagina. Autopsy reports showed the semen matched that found in the first victim. Martha had been racking her brain trying to find a common link between the victims. The fact that she was discussing the case in front of Towne on Thanksgiving was proof of how obsessed she'd become.

"It'll be good, though," Sheriff Booker said, "now that you've got some help. Are they working with you, or are the Feds pulling that holier-than-thou shit they're so famous for?"

"I'm trying to keep an open mind, Tom. But they spent two whole days pumping me for information, and now when I ask them something, they clam up. Johnson, that's the one still going through puberty, gave me some shit about running a parallel investigation. What they're doing, though, is re-doing everything I've already done. Makes me look stupid. And what's worse, Captain Grimes is practically drooling over these guys. I've never seen him so excited. We're talking some major ass-kissing going on. Meanwhile, he's taken away what little help I had. He reassigned Langly last week. I guess he figures now that the real experts are here, my role's not important." Martha was trying diligently to suppress her fury. She took a long swallow of beer.

I squeezed her waist, surprised to feel the hip holster beneath her blazer. It was Thanksgiving, after all. But ever since she'd been promoted to detective, she seemed to be on call nonstop. Still, it seemed silly to be wearing a gun on Thanksgiving. Mine was safe at home, hanging next to a purse I hadn't carried in over a year.

"What did they say about the college girl?" Booker asked.

"What college girl?" I asked. It irked me that Booker seemed to know more about these cases than I did. Obviously Martha had been confiding in him instead of me.

"Last week another kid from the community college turned up dead," Martha explained.

"A third victim? Why didn't I hear about this? I mean, why wasn't it in the news?" What I really wanted to ask was, why hadn't she told me instead of Booker?

"The girl wasn't necessarily murdered," Booker explained. "She was found on the beach, drowned. There's no reason to believe there's any connection to the serial murders. Martha was just mentioning the other day how odd it was for two kids from the same school to end up dying in such a short timespan."

"I read about that," Towne said. Even in the brisk autumn air, Towne was wearing a cotton T-shirt, and I marveled at the lack of goose bumps on his finely muscled arms. Towne was a Nautilus buff and worked out five days a week. "A body like Adonis, and a face like Godzilla," he liked to say about himself, referring to the pockmarks he carried with him as testimony to his agonizing teenage acne.

"I tried to get the Feds to look into it," Martha said, answering Booker's question. "They looked at me like I was some kind of moron. Johnson started going into a sermon about M.O.s and signatures. Like way out here in little ol' Kings Harbor we hadn't heard of such things. Like I was too stupid to realize that a killer who mutilates, rapes and strangles his victims and then inserts sperm-filled condoms in their vaginas as a parting gift, isn't suddenly going to wake up one day and decide he prefers to simply drown them."

"So they're not even going to look into it?" Booker asked.

"They don't believe there's anything to look in *to*. They weren't even interested in the autopsy report." For the first time, her brown eyes took on something other than anger. I recognized that look. Martha was up to something. Booker must have seen it too.

"I don't suppose the autopsy revealed anything of interest?" he asked. His moustache was twitching again.

"Well, she did drown, as suspected, but the coroner suspects she had sex before she did. There was no trace of semen, but she did have some pubic hairs mixed with hers. She also had a pretty hefty dose of Rohypnol in her system," she stated.

"Ro-what?" Towne asked.

"Better known in the college circuit as 'roofies,' " Martha explained. "Down south they call them roches."

"What's a roofie?" I asked.

"It's an illegal sedative. Around here they come in small, white tablets. They don't leave any taste or odor and they're cheap. Mixed with alcohol, they're the quickest way to getting smashed. And Lisa Lane also had a point-one-four alcohol count. Could, of course, mean nothing. But we know the killer likes his victims subdued. Both of his victims had at least some trace of chloroform in their systems. I'd say poor Lisa Lane was pretty subdued before she decided to go for a swim in the ocean that night. In pretty frigid temperatures, I might add."

"The paper said the kids had been partying in the dunes," Towne said. "That's not unusual, even this time of year. Even I've gone swimming in the winter, though I have to admit, I've never stayed in for more than a couple of minutes." Towne looked at his watch again, something he'd been doing off and on for the last hour.

"If that thing isn't done soon, I'll eat it raw. The smell is driving me nuts," Booker said.

"It's not a smell," Towne insisted. "It's an aroma. And it's supposed to drive you nuts. That's the point of standing around the barbecue. And it will be done in exactly seven and a half minutes." Towne may have looked like a lumberjack, but by profession he was an accountant,

8

and was notoriously meticulous and punctual. Rick, his gorgeous, slightly built, artistic lover who was inside cooking, was his complete physical and emotional opposite. They made a charming couple.

"The thing that's bugging me, I guess," Martha said sighing, "is the coincidence. I mean, what are the chances, do you think, of two girls going to the same little college, in the same drama department, both dying within six months of each other? I mean, they knew each other. That's the thing I keep coming back to. I don't care what the FBI says. I don't believe in coincidence."

Towne reached over and affectionately smoothed Martha's short brown hair behind one ear.

"It's a small town, Martha. Half the citizenry knows one another. Don't get mad at me, but I just don't see where one girl's being murdered has anything at all to do with another girl's drowning."

Martha patted Towne's hand and sighed. "I know. I know. But I can't shake this feeling I've got, and I don't know how to explain it. I certainly can't go to the FBI with a feeling. I mentioned it to Grimes and he about laughed me out of the office."

"I still say it's too bad you can't get someone in there undercover," Booker said. "Just to get a feel for things. Hell, someone posing as one of the drama students could probably find out more in a week than the police could in a month. At the very least it would serve to rule out any connection. That way, you could concentrate your efforts elsewhere."

"Grimes would never go for it," Martha said. "He's already dismissed the drowning victim as an unrelated case. Not to mention a closed case. Even if we had someone who could pass as a college student, who could kind of work their way into the same social circle those two girls were in, I'd never get his okay. Besides, most of the students there are straight out of high school. We don't have anyone on the force young enough to pull it off."

A brief look passed between Booker and Martha, so quick I almost missed it. For a second, it didn't register, and then, with a suddenness that made me nearly cough on my beer, I understood.

"Just tell me one thing," I said, laughing. "Which one of you thought this up?"

Booker raised his eyebrows, feigning total innocence, but Martha's face took on a pinkish hue.

"What?" Towne asked, looking confused.

"They want me to go undercover," I explained. "They want a thirty-two-year-old P.I. to pose as a college student. For free," I added.

"You could pass," Booker said. "Hell, half the time you don't look a day over twenty."

I thought about this, trying to look mad. "How old do I look the rest of the time?"

"It's probably a dumb idea," Martha said. "I mean, even if you could pull it off, it would probably just be a big waste of time. It's just that, with Langly being pulled off the case and all, I don't have any time to pursue the college angle. I just hate to leave this thing hanging."

Actually, the idea of working a new case intrigued me. Especially one that might be important. I was tired of following unfaithful husbands around with my zoom lens, hoping for a closeup shot proving their infidelity to the suspecting wife. Besides, anything would be better than sitting around moping over Maggie Carradine.

Suddenly, I wondered if Martha hadn't just made up this whole college-connection thing for that very reason. I looked at her, but her eyes revealed nothing. Would she do that? I wondered. Make up a bogus case just to keep me occupied? Just to help me survive a broken heart? She would, I decided. Which was one reason I loved her. But I doubted that's what she was doing now.

Suddenly, Towne's watch began to chirp.

"Get the door!" he ordered. Martha rushed to the glass slider, giving me a "we'll talk later" look.

10

"Hold the platter!" Towne said to Booker.

"Finally," Booker muttered.

"Cassidy, behold. Is this, or is this not, the most beautiful, perfectly cooked Thanksgiving turkey you have ever laid your eyes on?" Towne lifted the black lid off the Weber, revealing the golden brown bird beneath and, my mouth watering, I had to admit, it was.

Chapter Three

The table was a work of art. Rick had used all his fancy china and silver, and Booker's wife, Rosie, had contributed a beautiful lace tablecloth which her great-grandmother had brought over from Spain. Tina was filling the wine glasses, Towne was carving the turkey, and Rick and Rosie were bringing out bowls and platters by the armload. I wasn't used to being waited on, and it was kind of nice. Because I love to cook, I'm usually the one who ends up in the kitchen.

"You realize, of course, who'll be doing all the dishes," Booker said, winking at Martha and me.

"It'll be worth it," Martha said. Martha, who hardly ever cooked but who loved fine food, did the dishes a lot.

"You obviously haven't seen the kitchen," Tina teased, kissing Martha's cheek as she filled her glass. She was a slender, coffee-skinned woman with huge almond eyes and short cropped hair. I thought she looked like a model and told her so often. Martha was as smitten as she'd ever been, and even I was beginning to think she'd finally found someone to settle down with. Officially, they still had separate places, but the last time I'd been over to visit, I'd noticed a good deal of Tina's personal belongings scattered about Martha's condo.

When at last everyone had settled down and all the food had been heaped onto plates, Rick raised his glass for a toast.

"To the best friends a person could have," he said.

"To the cooks!" Booker replied.

"To family," Martha said. We clinked glasses, sipped the wine and dug in.

For once in my life, despite the fact that I was famished, I was having trouble eating. My throat had tightened up, and I was finding it difficult to swallow. I knew what Martha had just said was true. We were family. These were the people I loved. So why was I feeling so miserable?

I looked around the table. Martha and Tina were radiant with their mutual infatuation, Rick and Towne were as perfectly suited as two complete opposites could be, and Tom and Rosie were the most happily married straight couple I knew. And here I was, Cassidy James, a supposedly attractive, intelligent woman, alone on Thanksgiving.

Well, not alone, of course. But without the person I'd begun to consider my own Significant Other. It still hurt.

Four months had passed, and I still raced to the phone every time it rang, hoping it would be Maggie Carradine.

Sometimes it was, which only made it worse. Because instead of being ten miles away in Kings Harbor, she was calling me from Paris, France. And instead of calling to say she was coming home, she would say how important it was that she had gone, how there was so much unfinished business between her and Cecily, how being there and helping Cecily through the dying process was teaching Maggie so much about her own life.

I knew in my heart that what Maggie was doing was a truly noble thing. Part of me was proud of her. I, too, had watched a lover die, and I wouldn't wish that pain, that unbearable helplessness, on anyone.

But part of me was devastated. I knew this was uncharitably selfish, but I couldn't help it. Maggie had scarcely even mentioned this Cecily person. Sure, I'd seen the pictures: Cecily on water skis, the white spray splashing her tan, laughing face; Cecily throwing a snowball, her bright eyes beaming at the camera. But whenever I asked about her, Maggie clammed up. I sensed deep hurt and always backed off. I trusted that in time she'd be able to talk about it.

But I hadn't expected this. When I first broke the news to Martha, her brown eyes went wide with disbelief.

"She just up and left you?"

"Her ex-lover is dying," I said. I was trying hard to sound like someone who wasn't falling apart.

"But there must be someone else who could take care of her!" Martha had always idolized Maggie so I was surprised by her outrage.

"She wants to be there," I said. Just saying it made the lump in my throat swell.

"For how long?" Martha asked.

I'd asked the same silly question. Maggie had just looked at me, her eyes so infinitely sad that I felt I would suffocate.

"This is something I've got to do, Cass. I can't explain it and I can't justify it. I can't ask you to wait for me and

14

I won't blame you if you don't. You know how I feel about you. But this isn't about us. Cecily is unfinished business. We never had closure and it's haunted us both. I always figured that in time we'd find a way to wrap it up. Now I realize there's never going to be another time. This is something I just have to do."

There wasn't really anything I could say. I told her I understood. I told her I'd be here and that she could call me whenever she wanted but I'd understand if she didn't.

Of course, this turned out to be a big lie. When Maggie didn't call, I was devastated. When she did call, I felt even worse. I tried to sound cheerful and supportive, but in reality I felt lonely and abandoned. And then, out of the blue, Cecily went into some sort of remission.

I was ecstatic! If Cecily was well, Maggie could come home!

"She wants to go to Switzerland," Maggie said, her own excitement coming over the miles between us.

"Uh huh?" Caution had crept into my voice.

"The cancer isn't gone, Cass. The doctor says there's no telling how long this reprieve will last. Right now she feels good. I'm going to take her."

"Are you sleeping with her?" The second the words left my lips I wanted to take them back. I'd had no intention of ever asking this, though I'd been wondering for months. My heart pounded and my cheeks burned through the long silence.

"I'll call you when we're back," she said. I cradled the buzzing receiver against my cheek as tears fought their way to the surface. I should never have asked that question. Because the truth was, I didn't really want to know the answer.

Through it all, I tried to carry on as if nothing were wrong, but Martha was concerned. She'd known me since college and sensed I was hurting. Lately she'd quit trying to convince me that Maggie would be back. I think she was starting to doubt it herself.

Even Rick, the eternal optimist, had quit mentioning Maggie's name in my presence. The only one who still talked about her was Booker, and that was mostly out of guilt. He'd been fairly instrumental in keeping us together back when Erica Trinidad had threatened to sweep me off my feet. He'd convinced me to let Erica go and to dedicate myself to Maggie. And now Maggie had gone off to Switzerland with her first love, and I was left battling emotions I'd never even known I had.

"You're not eating!" Rick scolded.

"You've hardly touched a thing," Rosie said. "You're not coming down with something, are you?"

I was about to offer some feeble excuse when Martha's pager went off.

"Not on Thanksgiving," Tina said, looking worried. But Martha was already moving toward the phone. When she came back in, her face was grim, her voice tight.

"They just found Number Three," she said. "In Lincoln City."

Chapter Four

He'd watched her go inside, waited for the light to go on upstairs. Then he counted to himself. *One thousand one, one thousand two* ... *Now she's taking off her shoes, one thousand three, one thousand four, now she's running water for — the bath!* He giggled, imagining it, and willed himself to be patient, hardly able to contain the building excitement. He was parked across the street, the flowers clutched tightly in his sweaty palm, a handkerchief soaked with chloroform safely tucked inside the little jar in his jacket pocket.

The roses had cost him twenty dollars. Red roses with white baby's breath. He'd bought them in Kings Harbor and they were already starting to droop, but that hardly mattered. They were his pass key. Once he was inside, they were nothing.

When he reached one hundred, he opened the door and stepped out into the drizzle. The street was dark and deserted and the sky was the color of a dull knife blade. He turned up his collar and crossed the street to her house. His stomach was in knots. If this didn't work, he'd have to start over. He'd have to find someone new in a different town. It had happened before. He got irritated just thinking about it. He didn't want to start over and he didn't want someone new. He wanted this one. Right now. This was his Thanksgiving present to himself. It was, after all, Thanksgiving eve.

When she opened the door, he quickly replaced the expression on his face with one of cheerful kindness.

"Flower delivery for Miss Thompson?"

"I'm Sally Thompson," the young woman said, brows furrowed. He didn't allow himself more than a quick peek at her bathrobe. He'd been right. She'd been about to take a bath. Would've been the last one, at any rate. He almost felt bad that she was going to miss it. That's the kind of guy he was. He handed her the roses.

"If you'll just sign here," he said, handing her a clipboard. As he expected, she seemed confused about what to do with the roses. She couldn't hold the clipboard and sign her name with the roses still clutched in her hand.

"Here," he offered. He reached out and with surprising speed shoved the soaking wet handkerchief into her nose, at the same time pushing her inside the entryway. She struggled to get away, but the chloroform worked quickly. Her eyes rolled back in her head as he gently eased her down onto the floor.

It had taken less than a minute. To anyone passing by, he was nothing more than a prospective suitor, bringing roses to his girl on the day before Thanksgiving. If anyone had passed by, though he knew no one had. The street was *dark and silent. He stepped back out and walked briskly across the street, not even minding the rain that trickled down his neck. He whistled, feeling inordinately pleased with himself. Once he got her in the van, the real fun could begin.*

Chapter Five

The phone woke me at five-thirty. My heart slammed awake before the rest of me, and as I reached for the receiver, all I could think of was that the call might be from Maggie. It wasn't. Martha's husky voice came over the line.

"I know I woke you and I apologize. Have you got a pen?"

"Good morning to you too. What are you doing up so early? And yes, I have a pen. Somewhere." I dug around in my nightstand and found one. It was still dark outside, and the rain, which hadn't let up all night, was still plinking against the windowpanes.

"I'm not up early. I'm up late. The rain has made this a very tricky crime scene. Plus, the teenager posing as an FBI agent is not only slow and methodical, he's hung up on procedure. I thought I knew what red tape was. Ha! Don't say anything to hurt my feelings. I'm in such a bad mood as it is, I'm liable to start crying any minute."

"You haven't gone to bed yet? Oh, Martha. Tell me what you need. I'm wide awake." This wasn't entirely true, but she sounded so vulnerable, I'd have done anything.

"I thought I'd have more time to talk you into this, but given the circumstances . . ."

"Just tell me, Martha."

"Okay, listen up. I want you to go undercover like we discussed last night." A trickle of fear, or maybe excitement, worked its way down toward my stomach. "Come on, Cass. You need this case as much as I need you to work it. I saw it in your eyes last night. You're dying to get involved. And now with what's happened up here, I won't have one second to spend on it myself."

"What exactly did happen up there?" My pulse quickened.

"I can't say much. Same M.O. as the other two. If anything, he's getting more savage. Bastard's got a real thing for biting. We'll know more when we get the lab reports back. I'll have to wait to fill you in on the details. In the meantime, I've sort of unofficially enrolled you at the community college."

"Unofficially enrolled? What's that mean?"

"You remember that redhead I used to date? Darlene Meyers? She's the dean at KHCC. She pulled a few strings for me and starting Monday, you're going to be the new T.A. for the drama professor, a Dr. Monroe. Same one who teaches the class that both the drowning victim, Lisa Lane, and the first murder victim were in. Not bad, huh?"

"A T.A.?"

"Yeah, you know. Teaching assistant. According to Darlene, the real one dropped out a few weeks ago to get married, so this is perfect."

"You don't think people will be suspicious when I suddenly show up three-fourths of the way through the semester?"

"If anyone asks, you can tell them you've been T.A.ing for a night class, but your work hours changed or something. You'll think of something, Cass. It's the best I could do."

"Martha, when the hell did you have time to arrange this?"

"Day before yesterday." At least she had the good sense to sound contrite. "If you'd said no, it wouldn't have been that big a deal to cancel. I took a chance. Look, if you don't want to do it, I'll understand."

I didn't know whether to laugh or get mad. I pictured Martha, standing in a phone booth in the pouring rain a hundred miles away in Lincoln City, and decided to let it ride. "What exactly is it you'd like me to find out?" I asked.

Her sigh on the other end was pronounced. "I wish I knew, Cass. Just look and listen. Poke around when and where you can. I have no idea if the angle's even worth pursuing, but I'd feel a lot better being able to rule it out. I just can't shake the feeling that there's something not right about Lisa Lane's drowning. If you could find out what she had in common with the first victim, who they both knew, maybe you'd get something to go on. I don't know, Cass. Just nose around!"

"Okay, Martha. You've got me. I'll give it a try."

"Great! I was hoping you'd say that. I got you a studio right on campus, which means you'll be able to keep your eye on things pretty easily. Or if you want, I guess you could commute, but . . ."

"It looks like you've thought of everything."

"Well, enough to get you started anyway." She allowed herself a small chuckle. "You'll have to figure out what to do with the beasts."

The beasts to which she was referring were two cats who were both curled up on the bed. Gammon, the portly one, had burrowed herself in my lap and was purring contentedly. Her sister, Panic, was happily biting my hair.

I took notes as she gave me the address of my new digs, the location of my drama class and a few other details like the fact that the apartment key was under the mat. I promised to call her as soon as I knew anything. When I hung up the phone, I sat staring out through the gloomy dawn at the lake wondering what I'd just gotten myself into.

I didn't actually move in until Sunday. I spent Friday tying up some loose ends on a case I'd just finished, paid bills and got my place ready for my absence. Then I spent Saturday getting myself ready. Despite Martha's impressive efficiency, there were still quite a few things I needed to do. For one thing, if I was going to pull off my ruse as a college kid, I needed to do something about my clothes. It was true what Booker had said about my looking young, but the truth was, I had no idea how college kids were dressing these days, and I didn't want to give myself away before I even started. The one time I'd been on the little college campus I'd noticed how young most of the students were. Many community colleges appeal to a more mature clientele but in Kings Harbor the student body seemed mostly younger. If there were any students in their thirties, I hadn't seen them.

I picked up the phone and called my good friend Jess Martin. I told him what I needed and he immediately put his twelve-year-old daughter on the phone. No one is more hip to fashion than a twelve- or thirteen-year-old, I thought. I'd taught junior high, once upon a time, and I knew Jessie could tell me more in ten minutes than I'd learn in a week by myself.

"Cassidy!" she squealed into the receiver.

She was a cute kid, all arms and legs, getting taller by the day. She was also too damn smart for her own good. Jess, at Maggie's urging, had enrolled her in the gifted program in Kings Harbor, and I hardly ever saw her anymore. With a pang, I realized I missed the little squirt.

"I need a fashion consultant," I said. I told her my dilemma.

"Uh, Cass. I'm not exactly the one to help you in that department. I pretty much stick to jeans."

"Yeah, but if I took you shopping, could you show me what the older kids wear?"

"You want to wear mini-skirts and crop tops?"

She had a point. "Surely they can't all wear that."

"Well, it depends on what group you're in. The stoners are into retro. Or you could do grunge."

"Huh?"

"What time can you pick me up?"

That's what I liked about Jessie. Right away she was able to discern that even her limited fashion-sense far exceeded my own.

We went to the mall, a whole sub-culture of its own, and I got a lesson in, among other things, humility. The last time I'd bought hip-huggers, I'd been two sizes skinnier.

"You need one of those belly bracelets," she said, standing back to study her creation. I was wearing a pair of baggy-legged, hip-hugging jeans with slightly belled bottoms that made me feel ridiculous but actually looked kind of cute. The bright pink sweatshirt she'd chosen to go with them only came mid-waist and clearly showed my navel.

"Maybe I should get a navel ring," I suggested. Jessie's

eyes went huge behind her owlish glasses. "I'm just kidding," I assured her.

She found one of the belly bracelets and brought it to me. "Try this," she commanded.

We both decided it was quite sexy.

"You need cloddy shoes," she said. "No one wears regular tennis shoes."

"I thought Birkenstocks were back in." I had lots of old Birkenstocks.

Jessie rolled her eyes and tugged me toward the escalator. We went to the cloddy shoe department and found a pair I wasn't too embarrassed to wear. Still, I felt like I was dressed for combat in a disco.

"Come on," she said, grabbing my hand and pulling me through the crowded mall. The Christmas shoppers were already out in full force and it wasn't even December. Plastic Santas lined the windows and Christmas carols blared from hidden speakers. Normally, I'd have avoided the mall at all costs this time of year, but Jessie was enjoying herself immensely. When she stopped at the Snip and Curl I pulled back. "Cass, you can't pass for a college student like that." She drew out the *that* into about six syllables.

"Like what?" I said, running my hand through my hair. It was a bit overgrown but still short and sassy, the way I liked it.

"You know. You look kind of like, who's that tomboy on the reruns of *Family*?"

"Buddy?" I asked, my voice suddenly small. I loved Buddy. I had a major crush on Kristy McNichol when that show came out. Jessie thought I looked like Buddy? I was delighted. Until I saw the look in her eyes.

"Yeah, her. I mean, if you were going undercover on the basketball team, it might work. But theater people tend to be a little more funky."

"Funky?" I said.

"I was trying to use a vernacular you could relate to." She pushed her glasses up onto the bridge of her nose and waited for me to challenge her on this. No question about it, I thought. The gifted program was ruining what used to be a wonderfully sweet child. She was becoming a world-class smart ass. Dutifully, with a sense of dread, I followed her into the Snip and Curl.

Forty-five minutes later I emerged, a changed woman. Jessie was beside herself with glee. "You know who you look like?" she said, skipping ahead of me.

"Sinead O'Connor?"

"Very funny, Cass. You may not believe this, but I do know who Sinead O'Connor is. I was thinking you look a little like Meg Ryan. It's cute. All you need are some long, dangly earrings and you're set. Of course, with your hair like that, you should be wearing at least some lipstick."

"Oh, no. No way."

Jessie was shaking her head.

"What?" I said.

"I just didn't expect you to be so caught up in stereotypes, that's all. You act as if putting on lipstick would somehow be an indignity to your lesbianism."

"My what?"

She stopped in her tracks and turned to face me. "Your lesbianism. Homosexuality. Gayness. You are still gay, aren't you?"

"You know your problem, Jess? Someone obviously told you that precocious was cute."

"They did," she said, grinning. "You!"

"Well, I lied."

She took off running and I didn't catch up with her until we were almost out of the mall. I was tempted to take up child abuse and smack her a good one, but instead I took her inside a Dunkin' Donuts and we gorged our-selves on deep-fried sugar.

"You should try it, though," she said, noisily slurping milk through a straw.

"What's that, kiddo?"

"The lipstick. I wouldn't want to wear it myself, but with your new cut, it would look good. I'd go for red. Although black and purple are still in in some circles. Even pink or peach would work. Still, I'd start with the red."

"Jessie, did I ever tell you you're a royal pain in the ass?"

She smiled, the same sweet smile she'd always had, the one that never failed to melt my heart, and I forgave her for everything. After all, I'd been a precocious, smart-ass kid myself once. In fact, if you talked to certain people, I hadn't outgrown the smart-ass part completely.

By Sunday morning, I was ready. I hopped into my blue Sea Swirl and motored across Rainbow Lake to the Cedar Hills Marina. Hardly a day went by that I didn't make this same trek, but somehow today felt different. I felt as if I were heading forth on an adventure, and there was no one at home to see me off. Worse, no one would be there waiting for my return. The sun, however, was finally poking through the thinning clouds and I wasn't about to let that kind of maudlin thinking ruin my mood.

The lake was jam-packed with northern birds. Those visiting for the winter seemed to coexist nicely with the year-round residents. There were ospreys and blue herons, black cormorants and gulls, ducks of every kind and geese. I'd seen a few bald eagles recently as well. There were kingfishers, woodpeckers, robins and jays. I was almost getting to the point where I wasn't embarrassed to admit I'd become an ardent bird-watcher. I had a well-worn copy of the *Peterson Field Guide to Western Birds* and spent more time throwing down my binoculars to leaf through the book than I did tossing out a fishing line. Funny how things change, I thought.

When I'd first moved into the cedar and glass house on Rainbow Lake, I'd been overwhelmed by the awesome fishing. Now, I only fished when I wanted trout or bass, or occasionally bluegill, for dinner. I never could bring myself to try for catfish. All those whiskers got to me.

The first year, I'd taken so many pictures of bears and deer, people said I should have bought stock in Kodak. Now, I had a salt lick in the backyard for the deer and spent hours thinking up creative ways to keep them out of my gardens.

In those days I didn't know a thing about boats. But since they were the only way I could get from my house to civilization, I now owned four of them and had learned enough rudimentary mechanics and boat maintenance to keep them running year-round.

I had fled California to get away from the pain of losing my first lover to cancer. I quit my teaching career and buried myself in a new life. I'd loved the notion of a house accessible only by boat. The truth was, I still did.

But whereas back then I'd relished the solitude the isolation afforded me, I now longed for company. Maggie's sudden, unexpected departure had left me lonely and confused. Not only that, I was beginning to feel wronged. I was, I decided as I putt-putted across the water that fine November morning, lonely, angry and sexually deprived. Not necessarily in that order.

I handed over my boat to Tommy, the marina attendant, and started hefting my bags onto the dock.

"You cut your hair!" he said, sounding accusatory.

"You don't like it?" I was going to kill Jessie — as soon as this case was over.

"I do. No, really. It just kinda took me by surprise. You know who you look like? That movie actress, Meg Ryan. Hell, Cassie. You could be in the movies."

God, I loved Tommy. He was a one-of-a-kind gem. He talked like a hillbilly, looked like one of Santa's elves and could always be counted on to come through in a pinch. In fact, he was one of the few people in the universe I'd come to trust.

"Do you think it makes me look younger?" I asked. I wasn't wearing my new duds. I just had on an old pair of Levi's and a ratty UCLA sweatshirt. Tommy stood back and gave me his full attention.

"Shoot," he finally decided, "I don't even know how old you look the regular way. How old are you, anyway?"

"Twenty-five," I tried, smiling innocently.

"Nah, no way. Really? Nah, you're funnin' me. Twenty-five? Jeez."

Somehow, this wasn't cheering me up. I changed the subject. "I'll be gone for a couple of days, Tommy. Keep an eye on the boat for me, will you?"

"Sure thing, Cass. I mean, Meg." He laughed merrily and grabbed one of my suitcases, carrying it up the ramp to my Jeep Cherokee.

When I pulled out onto Highway One for the short drive to Kings Harbor, I worked on trying to calm the butterflies in the pit of my stomach.

Chapter Six

Kings Harbor Community College sits on one of the nicest pieces of real estate in the Pacific Northwest. The grounds are covered with cedar and fir trees, and the softly rolling hills are blanketed with thick, plush grass. From the highest points, one can look out over the white sand dunes to the west and see peeks of the Pacific Ocean half a mile away. To the east lies the busy harbor for which the town is named.

I followed Martha's directions and found the tiny studio apartment she'd rented for me right on the edge of the campus. One look inside, and I knew why it had been available. I'd been in bathrooms bigger than this.

But it was clean enough, and the single bed was firm. There was a small mini-fridge, a two-burner stove and a sink the size of a large soup bowl. I didn't plan on spending a lot of time there anyway, I thought, cramming my clothes in the minuscule closet. I changed into one of my new outfits, told myself I didn't look as silly as I felt and took off on a self-guided tour of the campus.

The drama building was on the westernmost knoll of the campus, across a parking lot from the gymnasium. The lot was mostly empty on this Thanksgiving weekend, but the gym was open and I stuck my head in the doorway and watched a dozen young men playing basketball. The sound of tennis shoes squeaking on the hardwood floor brought back fond memories. Unfortunately, so did the smell of fresh sweat mixed with dirty socks.

With a sudden pang, I wished I could invite myself into the game, shoot some hoops with the boys. But I knew this was ridiculous. It had been years since I'd handled a basketball. Still, I knew if it had been a group of women playing, I'd have been tempted to join them.

Reluctantly, I tore myself away from the gym and strolled through the rest of the campus. It was a pretty school. The buildings were one-story brick rectangles with covered porticos along the fronts. Each building had its own lawn-covered quad with benches and tables strewn about. Here and there couples lounged, reading or studying in the unexpected sunshine. The whole school had a lazy, kick-back feeling to it. Not the kind of place one expected to find a serial killer, I thought. But maybe the perfect place for a killer to find a victim.

The library was about right for a community college. It was small but surprisingly busy for a holiday weekend. Kids hunched over word processors or sat slumped in chairs in front of reference tables taking copious notes. Others just appeared to be reading for pleasure.

The same feeling I'd had in the gym, something between longing and belonging, washed over me again. I'd loved college. I'd never wanted it to end. I loved the classes, the learning, the whole environment. And the women! Once I discovered my own preferences, it seemed that women were everywhere. UCLA had been crawling with potential lovers.

Of course, this wasn't exactly UCLA. I looked around at the students and smiled inwardly. Even here, I thought, there were a few likely looking lesbians. I shook my head and hurried back out into the sunlit day. I was in definite trouble if I was starting to look at eighteen-year-olds.

I spent the rest of the day acquainting myself with the surrounding neighborhood. After a quick check in the phone book for the address, I found the townhouse development that Lisa Lane had lived in. It was a small complex with single-story, white stucco dwellings. Although attached, they were fairly private. They even had their own driveways, and a cute white picket fence surrounded the tiny lawns in front, giving each little place a homey feeling. Some of the windows already sported Christmas lights and decorations, despite the fact it was still November. According to the phone book, Lisa Lane had lived in number three. On a whim, I knocked on her door. To my surprise, it opened.

"Yes?" The young woman standing in the doorway peered down at me with curiosity. She was a big-boned woman, and her baggy red sweats didn't quite conceal the large breasts and hips beneath.

"Uh, I heard there might be a townhouse available around here, but I didn't see any vacancy sign. Do you know which one it is?" I was winging it big-time.

"This whole complex is full up." She blew at her brown bangs. "Maybe what you heard was that there was a roommate opening." She eyed me suspiciously, her brown eyes squinting past the glare.

"That's it," I said. "Is this the right place?"

"You new? I haven't seen you around."

"No, I just don't get out much. Until recently I was

working days and taking classes at night. I've got a little studio over on Third, but it's really small. These places seem much nicer." I peeked around her into the room. "By the way, my name is Cassidy."

"I'm Rhonda. Rhonda Lou Whittaker. Come on in," she said, moving aside. "You might as well look around. I didn't pick up or anything. I wasn't expecting to show it, you know, until the first of the month. My old roommate was paid up until then. The rent's six-fifty, which is pretty steep, but it's only three twenty-five for half." Without warning, her hands flew to her face and she sank onto the tattered sofa and began to sob. I stood across from her, not sure what to do. Finally, she blew her nose into a wrinkled tissue and looked at me with tortured brown eyes. "I'm sorry," she said, sniffling. "That keeps happening. I think I'm okay, and then all of a sudden, wham, the dam breaks loose."

"You had a falling-out with your roommate?"

She shook her head impatiently, tears streaming down her face again. "She — she's dead," she managed through her sobs. One thing I was pretty sure of; this girl hadn't killed Lisa Lane. She was genuinely grief-stricken. Either that or guilt-ridden.

"What happened?" I sat down on the other end of the sofa and waited while she blew her nose.

"She drowned!"

I braced myself for another onslaught of tears, but she held them back. "That's terrible. When? How did it happen?"

"Two weeks ago Friday. She went out with her friends. She'd always do stuff like that, you know? Go out and stay up real late partying. I can't believe you didn't read about it in the paper." She looked up, suddenly embarrassed. "I'm sorry. I don't need to burden you with this."

"No, really. It helps to talk about these things. So, you're saying she liked to party?"

She nodded. "Even on weeknights sometimes. I always

33

told her to be careful. I mean, I was talking about something else entirely. I was worried she'd end up pregnant or with AIDS. I never dreamed something like this would happen." The tears slid out again, but she was doing her best to control them.

"How did she drown? Was it a swim party?"

"Oh, no. Nothing like that. They used to go out to the dunes. You know, to the beach. I guess she decided to go for a swim. No one remembers seeing her go in the water, though. Don't you think that's odd? Sure they were all stoned out of their minds, but still, you'd think someone would see her go into the water. When she didn't come home that night, I just knew something terrible had happened."

"What about her date? Didn't he wonder where she was?"

"Oh, she didn't really have an actual date. I mean, she had a major crush on this guy, Mark Lewis, and he was there that night, but it wasn't like the two of them went together. She got a ride there with Bridget, a friend of hers. Bridget says when she couldn't find Lisa, she just figured she'd gotten a ride home with someone else. The dune parties are that way. They're almost close enough to walk home, if you want to. It just makes me so sad to think of dying and no one even noticing you're gone." She started to sniffle into her sodden tissue again and got up to get a fresh one.

"Was she pretty?" I asked.

She turned to look at me through narrowed, puffy eyes. "Why would you want to know something like that?"

"Well, I just wondered. It sounds like she was popular and all. It doesn't matter, I guess."

"She was too pretty for her own good," she blurted. "What I mean by that is, she was always trying to starve herself. It's not like she needed to diet! She was skinny to start with. But she always wanted to be one size smaller. She practically lived on nonfat yogurt and carrot sticks. I

used to try to get her to eat real food, but she was kind
of obsessed that way. That must sound petty, saying that
now that she's gone."

"Not at all. I'm sure even Lisa had her faults."

"Well, to me, she was usually pretty nice. I think it's
because she didn't see me as competition, you know? I
didn't run in her circle. She was a lot more social than I
am. I'm kind of a bookworm."

"Speaking of books, did she keep a diary?"

Rhonda's brown eyes widened and she looked down at
her feet before meeting my gaze. "Lisa? Not that I knew
of." Suddenly, her eyes narrowed. "Why would you want to
know something like that?" Just like that, her tone had
gone from evasive to suspicious. For some reason, I got the
distinct impression she was lying.

"I just thought that if she had kept one, it might shed
some light on what happened that night, that's all. It must
be hard, not knowing exactly what happened."

"Do you want to see the rest of the place? Lisa's room
was the one in back. Her sister is coming next week to get
her stuff, so the room will be ready whenever you are."
She was obviously eager to change the subject.

I did a quick tour, wondering at Rhonda's deception
and wishing I could take more time with Lisa's belongings.
Her room was neat, except for the closet, which had
clothes crammed and stuffed into every inch of space.
There was a small bookshelf with a few dozen books on
the shelves, mostly textbooks. I glanced around for a diary
or journal, but knew that even if she had kept one, she
wouldn't keep it on an open shelf.

I thought back to my own college days, picturing my
tiny dorm room and the prying roommate who would have
loved to read my private thoughts. I'd kept my diary in my
underwear drawer beneath a false bottom that I'd
fashioned from a piece of particle board. But I couldn't
very well start going through Lisa's underwear drawer. I
sighed and quickly checked out the rest of the apartment.

There was just one bathroom, a small kitchen and a utility room which had been fashioned into a makeshift darkroom. I peeked into Rhonda's bedroom and then returned to the living room.

"It looks good," I said. "Who's the photographer?"

"Oh, it's just a hobby," she said. "So, do you think you're interested?" She seemed so anxious for a roommate that I suddenly felt guilty for this whole charade.

"I'll need to see if I can get the money together. It'll take some finagling, but it sure is a lot nicer than where I'm staying. You know, something just occurred to me. I know it's none of my business, but was Lisa depressed or anything? I mean, it just seems so weird that she'd go into the ocean by herself in the middle of the night."

"That's what the police asked," she said. "But I just told them the truth. As far as I know she wasn't upset about a single thing. She had gotten the lead in a play they were doing and was real excited about that. Like I said, she had a crush on this guy and he seemed interested too, so she was happy. Her grades were good. I mean, there wasn't anything bad going on in her life at all. Not that I knew about."

"But she was into drugs?"

"Oh, just recreational stuff. She tried to get me to smoke pot with her once, but I don't like the smoke. I don't think she did anything else. I was real surprised when the police said there were drugs in her system. Of course, everyone denies doing anything more than pot that night, but what are they going to say? 'Oh yes, Officer, we were all snorting cocaine'? Even the police knew they were lying. You're not into drugs, are you?"

"Oh, no," I assured her.

"Well, as long as you don't smoke inside or have any totally weird habits, if you want to, you can move in whenever you're ready. To tell you the truth, it's kind of spooky living alone."

I told her I'd let her know as soon as I could, then let

myself out, feeling like I'd made some progress. I knew the name of the boy Lisa had been seeing and the name of the girl she'd gone to the dunes with. Also, if Rhonda's assessment was accurate, I doubted Lisa had committed suicide that night. But most of all, something told me that Lisa Lane had kept a diary and that Rhonda Lou Whittaker knew where it was. It wasn't much, but it was a start.

I jaywalked across Harbor Drive and headed for an Italian restaurant I'd seen earlier called Mama Mangione's. It was early for dinner, but I'd skipped lunch and was famished after a whole day of exploring. I don't really like eating alone in restaurants, but considering the size of my new kitchen, I didn't think I'd be doing a whole lot of cooking.

I sat down in a corner booth, ordered a half-liter of Chianti and Mama's Early-Bird Special, which was manicotti. It came with garlic bread and salad. When my plate was scraped clean and my wineglass was empty, I headed for the College Market and bought a week's worth of absolute essentials, including a large bag of peanut M&M's.

Chapter Seven

On Monday morning the clouds were back, white billowy giants slugging across the sky, the ocean breeze pushing them eastward. I donned my hip-hugging jeans, new clodhopper boots and the navel-exposing sweatshirt. I studied my face. How young could I pass for? I wondered. The new dangling earrings worked well with my hair, I thought, and for the briefest moment I wondered if Jessie had been right about the lipstick. I banished the thought, gave myself one last cursory glance in the mirror and headed out onto campus.

I knew the drama class started at ten and filled a two-hour block. It met four days a week. Beyond that, I knew very little about what I was getting myself into.

I found a row of vending machines lining the entrance to the building and fed quarters into the slot that promised hot coffee. I scalded my tongue on something reminiscent of cleaning fluid and wrinkled my nose. I was startled by laughter behind me.

"That stuff will kill you," a wild-haired woman said, grinning.

"*Now* you tell me."

"You're safer getting the hot water and adding your own tea bag, although sometimes even the water comes out kind of funny."

"Thanks for the tip. You know where room PA one is?

"That's the Performing Arts building. You're already there. See those double doors? Just go on through, you can't miss it. You from the paper?"

"Huh?"

"The media. I just figured you were here to write an article on the play, no?" She was a short, stocky woman with black frizz worn like a halo around her head. Her eyes were bright and dark, making her seem wise beyond her probable eighteen or nineteen years.

"No. Actually, I'm the new T.A. for Dr. Monroe. The drama teacher?"

"No shit," she said. "Boy, we sure could use one. The last one jumped ship and things are getting crazy around here. You'll like Monroe. Probably work your ass off, though. She's kind of a workaholic. If you want to get off to a good start, you better come on. Class doesn't officially start till ten, but they've already been at it for an hour. We open in two weeks and we're about a million years away from being ready. I'm Rita, by the way. Rita Colby. Someday you can say you knew me when."

"Cassidy James," I said. I'd already decided that it was easier to use my real name. "Keep it simple," my old mentor, Jake Parcell, had always said. "Stay as close to the truth as you can." I tossed the still-full Styrofoam cup into a trash can and followed the energetic woman through the double doors.

I had to let my eyes adjust to the dark. Rita, seemingly unaffected by the sudden lack of light, moved down the aisle and disappeared backstage. I stood where I was and took in my surroundings.

Onstage, a dark-complected, good-looking boy with a shock of wavy black hair was dressed in a white caftan and delivering his lines with all the pomposity of a vaudeville actor. I was thinking he wasn't very good when suddenly, from the darkness to the left of the stage, music welled up and he began to sing. I hadn't realized the play was a musical. I listened to the lyrics and was further surprised to find them doing *Jesus Christ Superstar.* A rather ambitious undertaking for a community college, I thought.

But the boy, in the role of Judas, had an impressive voice. He belted out the lyrics with tremendous volume. His hand gestures were a bit grandiose, bordering on comical, but the booming bass reverberated in the small theater with astounding clarity. Suddenly the music stopped and a tall, thin, red-headed man wearing a black suit leaped onto the stage from the orchestra pit. His pale face was blotched with color, whether from heat or emotion I couldn't tell.

"Stop!" he commanded. "Stop, stop stop!"

The boy stopped mid-lyric and thrust his hands on his hips with exaggerated exasperation.

"Mr. Lewis, let me explain this again." The man stood at the edge of the stage and shook his finger at Judas. "You cannot just hit the notes and call it singing. There is a rhythm to this melody. It is the same rhythm every time. It will be there two weeks from now, when we open. *If* we open. It would be nice if you were singing to the same rhythm we were playing."

"I thought I was, Mr. Purvis," the boy said, putting a sarcastic emphasis on the *mister*. Even from where I stood, I could see the color in his cheeks.

The taller man put his arm on the boy's shoulder. "It would help if you listened to the music while you sang. Just try it. Okay?"

The boy shrugged the hand off his shoulder and folded his arms across his chest. Suddenly, a voice from the audience rang out, causing me to jump. I hadn't realized anyone was sitting there, a dozen feet away.

"Okay, everyone. Let's take five. Markie, you're doing fine. In fact, I've got an idea that might help. Come on up here for a moment, okay? And people, five means five. Not ten or fifteen. Got it?"

Someone turned on the houselights and the whole room changed as I got my first look at Dr. Monroe. She was wearing plaid pants, sensible loafers, a creamy silk blouse and a blue blazer that matched her eyes. Her blond hair was pulled up in some kind of a knot, with random little wisps falling down her neck and forehead. Her features weren't extraordinary by themselves, but put together, she was quite attractive. I watched as she put both hands on Markie's shoulders and leaned toward him, talking low but loud enough for me to hear.

"I think the problem is this," she said, looking right into his eyes. He stared back, apparently as mesmerized with her presence as I was. "This theater is so small, and your voice so well-developed, that I think it's difficult for you to hear the orchestra when you sing full-volume. But I've been thinking. You could probably sing three-quarters volume, and it would still be plenty loud enough for this room. And that way, you'll be able to hear the music better. What do you think?"

"I don't know if I can," he said, clearly pouting. "I never tried it."

"Well, this would be a good time to give it a try. You know, thinking about it, I bet you could tone down your gestures at the same time. Just make everything a little smaller, to better fit this small theater. Your voice, your mannerisms, even your facial expressions. You've got everything on full blast. Turn it all down a quarter-notch and see how it works. Okay?"

Markie nodded, his face and body beginning to regain the cocky confidence I'd seen when I first entered. When he walked back toward the stage, I heard her let out a relieved sigh.

"Excuse me. You wouldn't be Dr. Monroe by any chance." I smiled and offered her my hand.

"At the moment, I'm not entirely sure," she said, shaking my hand anyway. I realized too late that college kids probably didn't go around shaking their professors' hands.

"I'm Cassidy James, your new T.A." I smiled again and finally let go of her hand. My fingers were humming.

She blinked. "You're kidding."

"Nope. Actually, I'm not officially enrolled until next semester, but the Dean said she could assure me the position then, if I was willing to fill in temporarily for a few weeks now. She said something about your other T.A. quitting?"

"Dropped out, unfortunately. Your timing couldn't be better! We're up to our ears in alligators here. How much do you know about the theater?"

"Uh, well . . ."

She cut me off, still looking hopeful. "You can't by any chance sew, can you?" I hated to let her down.

"I'm a fast learner," I said.

She laughed, a good, full-throated sound that sent tingles down my extremities. "I like that. You'll do fine. Pull up a chair."

I sat one seat away from her and watched for nearly two hours as she alternately praised, cajoled and coaxed her students into action. It didn't take long to notice the slightly adversarial relationship between the orchestra conductor and her. It was as if they were playing good cop, bad cop. He tore them down, she built them back up. It worked so well, I wondered if it was something they'd rehearsed.

While I watched, I wondered how I was going to approach Markie, the baritone Judas, about Lisa Lane. I couldn't just walk up to him and start firing questions. Somehow I was going to have to get myself invited into the little social circle Rhonda had told me about.

Something else I wondered about was the buxom beauty who'd taken Lisa's lead part. Rhonda had said that Lisa had played Mary Magdalene. If so, it hadn't taken her replacement very long to learn the lines. Of course, she'd probably been the understudy all along.

Still, it made me wonder. Would somebody kill out of envy over a starring role at a community college? If Mary Jane had killed Lisa, it pretty much ruled out any connection between Lisa's death and the other victims'. I just couldn't see the serial killer being a woman. In fact, I wasn't convinced Lisa Lane had been killed at all. But Martha said she had a "feeling" and I owed it to her to find out everything I could.

Besides, I wasn't entirely sorry I was there. Sitting in the dark next to a likable and rather sexy director and watching college kids strut their stuff onstage wasn't such a bad way to spend a Monday morning.

"Okay, people. Let's call it a day," Dr. Monroe shouted.

Right away the houselights came up and people started scrambling around in all directions. For the first time, I saw the people behind the horns and strings. The kids in the orchestra looked a completely different lot than the actors. More serious, yet somehow less worldly. I doubted the two groups intermingled socially.

"Well, what do you think?" Dr. Monroe asked, standing to stretch.

"I think two weeks from now will be here sooner than you think."

43

She let out another rich, throaty laugh and shook her head. "I knew I liked you. You don't mince words. Come on, I'll introduce you around."

I followed her down the aisle toward the orchestra pit where Mr. Purvis was folding sheet music into a black case.

"Good news, Mr. Purvis. The gods have sent us help. Meet Cassidy, my new T.A."

"You don't say," he said, lifting a pale orange eyebrow in my direction. His thick, black-rimmed glasses were fogged up and there was a fine film of perspiration on his freckled brow. He dabbed at it self-consciously. "We sure can use you," he said, smoothing his orangeish hair back from his forehead. The dampness had caused it to spring up in unruly tufts.

"Just tell me where to start."

"You can't sing, can you?" His smile was small and tight, as if concerned about hurting Dr. Monroe's feelings, but a few of the orchestra members laughed aloud at the private joke, and Dr. Monroe returned the smile.

"I'm going to get her started on those costumes," she said, taking my arm. She steered me away from the cackling group.

"He doesn't seem too pleased with the actors," I pointed out.

"Opening-day jitters," she whispered. "This is his first play. Mine too, for that matter."

"Really?" I looked at her, surprised.

"You couldn't tell?"

"I thought you did a great job today," I said. "You soothed their egos, kept the pace going, only interrupted when it seemed absolutely necessary and kicked their butts at the right times. I figured you've been doing this forever."

She laughed. "Thank you. I think. Are you always this observant?" Her blue eyes smiled and she tucked a stray blonde wisp behind her ear. "Actually, I'm an English lit professor. This is, well, just a temporary assignment. I thought it might be fun. What did I know?" She laughed again and led me backstage.

We were greeted with general confusion and noise. People were changing into their street clothes right in front of one another. Costumes were flung around the room along with an assortment of props. The place was a mess.

"Listen up, everyone. This is our new T.A., Cassidy. She's going to give me the last-minute help I need to get the costumes and props in order. So before you leave today, everything needs to be put back where it's supposed to go. Those of you I talked to about alterations, be so kind as to put your costumes in that box next to Mary Jane. Markie, please. Nobody's interested in seeing you in your under-shorts right now. That's what these partitions are for. Brad, did you have a question?"

Brad, the blond-headed, surfer type who played Jesus, had his hand raised tentatively. "Are you going to talk to Roland about cutting off everyone's lines?"

What was it, I wondered, that made so many surfer-types talk through their nose? I looked around and spotted Roland, the chubby boy who played Pontius Pilate. His cheeks were pudgy and pink and his brown bangs were cut short, giving him a Julius Caesar look. He'd been a good singer, with a high, refined voice, but it was true, he did tend to cut off other people's lines.

"I'm sure nobody is intentionally cutting off anyone else's lines, Brad. We're all trying as hard as we can. Right, Roland?"

The boy nodded, his big eyes grateful pools of brown.

"Mary Jane, can I see you a moment?"

The girl who'd taken Lisa's place as Mary Magdalene was busily brushing her long brown curls. From the audience, I had noticed her distinctive figure with its narrow waist and full bosom. Now, in street clothes she wore a skimpy crop top that barely covered her breasts, which she seemed to thrust forward as she walked.

Dr. Monroe spoke in a low voice so the others couldn't hear. "Mary Jane, I think we're going to have to change that opening number a little. Tone down the sexy part. It's a little distracting."

"But she's a whore!" Mary Jane cried. Her dark eyes widened innocently. "I thought that was the whole point. She's a whore, but Jesus loves her anyway. How will the audience know she's a prostitute unless I play it that way?"

"Think of it like this," the professor said, putting her arm around Mary Jane and walking her farther away from the others. I trailed behind them. "She's a prostitute by profession, but that doesn't make her a bad person. She loves Jesus with her whole heart. It's true that she uses her body for money, but that's the only way she can get by. She's not just coming on to Jesus. She has real feelings for him. And he has real feelings for her. The foot-rub scene should be as much a comforting thing as a seduction."

Mary Jane looked ready to cry. "I was *trying* to make it a comforting thing," she wailed. "Why is it that everyone always thinks I'm trying to act sexy? I'm not!" Her lower lip had started to quiver and her shoulders shook, causing her thrust-forward breasts to jiggle violently. Suddenly, all eyes seemed to be riveted on the unfolding scene, including mine.

"You're doing fine," Dr. Monroe said, patting Mary Jane's back. "I think if you start thinking of her as a poor, downtrodden woman forced into the only profession available to women at the time, rather than as a shameless hussy, it will all come together."

Mary Jane managed to stifle what seemed an impending sob, then nodded. "Other than that, did I do okay?"

"You did fine," the professor assured her. We both watched Mary Jane sashay out of the room, and I couldn't help but notice that we weren't the only ones watching. It was hard to ignore her retreating derriere.

"Do you suppose she practices that?" I whispered.

Dr. Monroe glanced at me, somewhat startled. Her blue eyes appraised me curiously and I realized I hadn't been acting much like a student. But it was too late to take it back. To my relief, she grinned. "It can't be natural," she admitted in a whisper. "An overabundance of Y chromosomes perhaps? She's quite a change from the first Mary Magdalene, I'll say that."

"What happened to the first one?" I was relieved that I wasn't going to have to change my basic personality for this role. It was going to be hard enough just gathering information without also having to put on a big act. We walked through a doorway to a large prop room where a pile of unpainted flats were stacked against the wall.

"You don't know?" she asked. I shook my head and she let out a heavy sigh. "I'm sorry I even brought it up. Her name was Lisa and she died a couple of weeks ago. It was a shock to us all. She drowned in the ocean less than a mile from here. The kids are pretty torn up about it. That's why we're so far behind schedule. I just couldn't bring myself to hold rehearsals." She paused, and let out another sigh before continuing. "Lisa had been dating Markie, the one who plays Judas. Mary Jane was her understudy. I was ready to cancel the whole thing, but the kids voted to go on. They say that's what Lisa would have wanted." She leaned against the wall and blew a blond wisp from her eyes. "Poor Mary Jane has been under tremendous pressure. Not just to learn all the lines and staging practically overnight, but to have to fill in for someone they were all so close to. If people seem a little on edge around here, you can understand why. It's been a nightmare for all of us. Especially with this coming on top of what happened to poor Sarah Ringer last June."

"Sarah Ringer?" I asked, my pulse racing.

She looked at me sharply, then her shoulders slumped with fatigue. You don't read the papers?"

"I'm new to town. This is my first semester. What happened?"

"Another one of the drama kids died last summer," she said. "Only, that one was murdered. She was such a headstrong, gutsy kid. I really liked her. Everyone did. It was horrible. They still haven't caught the guy. It really spooked the whole community. We were going to do *Bye Bye Birdie* for summer stock but I canceled the show. Contrary to popular belief, sometimes the show doesn't go on." Her eyes, which had been so full of life just moments before, looked tired and troubled. "I'm sorry to dump all of this on you, but as long as you're part of the cast, you might as well know."

"No wonder everyone looks ready to crack," I said. "I thought Markie was going to lose it when Mr. Purvis jumped all over him. And then poor Pontius Pilate looked like he might cry when Jesus accused him of cutting off everyone's lines, and now Mary Jane is all upset for being too sexy. I thought maybe theater people were just an emotional lot. But considering the circumstances, I'd say you're all doing remarkably well."

"See these flats?" she asked, changing the subject abruptly. I glanced at her and was surprised to find her troubled eyes had welled up. "I'd like you to make these black. There's paint in the cupboard, along with brushes, rollers, drop cloths and whatever else you might need. You *can* paint?"

"Like Picasso," I said, grinning. I found myself really wanting to help this woman, or at least cheer her up. "I can start now, if you want."

"Don't you have another class to get to?"

"Actually, no. I've been working days and taking a few classes at night until my day job ended. At the moment, I've got plenty of free time."

"Really?"

I smiled and nodded. "Just put me to work. I'm all yours."

"Well, if you really mean it, what I'd really like is help with those costumes. These flats can wait until tomorrow, but I'd like to have the costumes done today. I've got my sewing stuff all set up in my living room, if you don't mind walking a few blocks."

I assured her it would be my pleasure, and we headed back to the dressing room. I was surprised to see it had been so quickly deserted.

"Lunchtime," she explained. "They're probably all down at the Pizzaria. In fact, I'm half-starved myself. Why don't we grab a Subway on the way to my place. My treat."

It was another twenty minutes before we managed to get out. There were doors to lock, clothes to hang, props to move and bundles of costumes to gather. She piled them into my arms, and I followed her out into what had become a nice day. The clouds had all blown inland. And despite the fact that I knew little more about the case than I had that morning, I was feeling cheerfully optimistic.

Chapter Eight

It had been less than a week since his Thanksgiving eve date with Sally Thompson and already he was starting to itch with the desire for a new encounter. But it was too soon. He must exercise control. There was only one way to quell the trembling inside. He closed his eyes and let himself remember . . .

He was kneeling above her, listening to her breathe. The sound was getting stronger now, growing more regular, and

*this excited him. Soon she'd open her eyes and see him.
And scream.*

He smiled, licked his lips and waited.

He played the scene over and over.

Chapter Nine

The professor's townhouse was on the same side of the campus as mine, but a few blocks north and in a much nicer location. Situated on a knoll, it faced west toward the towering white dunes that led to the ocean.

"Nice view," I said, standing at the bay window and looking out past the spruce and fir to the rolling white mounds.

"Yes, it makes it worth it," she said. "Living right on the edge of campus has its drawbacks, but I do love looking out that window. Give me a few seconds and I'll be right out. I want to change." She disappeared down a hallway, and I was left to do a little surreptitious snooping.

It was a small house, but nicely appointed. There was a good-sized kitchen, a small dining room which had been turned into a temporary sewing area, and a small but comfortable living room. I peeked down the hallway and counted doors. There were only two bedrooms and no sign of a roommate.

Along one wall of the living room was an étagerè with a stereo system, television, VCR and assorted knickknacks on the shelves. Among them was a framed picture of the professor with her arm around a young, good-looking man. They were at the beach, and the camera had caught them laughing, their blond hair tousled by the wind, their faces sunburned and glowing. I found myself staring at the picture, disappointed. I hated to admit it, but I had let myself entertain the notion that the professor might be gay. A bad habit, I told myself. I was getting to be more like Martha every day.

"Kick off your shoes, make yourself at home," she said, startling me. She had changed into a pair of khaki trousers and an oversized navy velour pullover. She wore fuzzy white golf socks on her feet that made her seem vulnerable. I looked down at my new shoes and decided she was right. I'd never be comfortable sitting around in those clodhoppers. I slipped them off and set them by the door.

"Have you lived here long, Dr. Monroe?" I asked, watching her place two pepperoncini next to the sandwich on each paper plate.

"Please, you can't sit around in your bare stockings and call me Dr. Monroe. My name is Lauren. Is Diet Coke okay?"

I nodded. She handed me a plate and I followed her to the table which was three quarters covered with fabric.

"Just move it out of the way," she said, shoving a pile onto the floor. "I've only been here since last spring. I'm on a sabbatical from Stanford. That's why I decided just to rent." She seemed embarrassed by the modest apartment.

She should see the place I was staying in, I thought, taking a tentative bite of the dripping sandwich. She had insisted I order the vegetarian special, and one bite told me she had done me a favor.

"It's none of my business," I said, trying not to talk with my mouth full, "but what could possibly entice an English lit professor to leave a first-rate university like Stanford to come out to a community college in Kings Harbor, Oregon?"

She studied me for a minute and took another bite. A dollop of olive oil had dripped onto her chin and I had a ridiculous urge to reach over and wipe it off with my finger. I shook the image from my head and waited for her to answer.

"My brother is dying," she said at last. "I don't know how much time he has, but I wanted to be here with him. That's really all there is to it."

I suddenly felt at a loss for words. Our eyes met briefly before we both looked away. We ate for a while in silence.

"It must have been difficult for you to just pick up and leave your whole life behind," I said at last. I knew I wasn't thinking of her; I was thinking of Maggie.

"Not as hard as you might think. There really weren't that many attachments." She dabbed at the oil on her chin.

"No husband, then?" I was prying shamelessly.

She laughed at my straightforwardness. "No. No husband." She had a look on her face I couldn't read.

"I saw the photo," I said. "On the shelf. I thought maybe he was your husband." I couldn't help myself. I was out of control.

She smiled ruefully. "That's Corey, my brother. His friend Pete took that picture last year when I came to visit. That was before his T cells started dropping like flies. I'm afraid he'll never look that good again."

"AIDS?" I asked unnecessarily. The only people I'd ever

54

known to discuss their T cells were battling AIDS. She nodded, pushing the remains of her sandwich aside.

"Well, if we don't get started, we'll never have these costumes finished in time for tomorrow's dress rehearsal." She seemed anxious to change the subject and I couldn't blame her. I helped her clear our lunch plates from the table. "You can start with these hems," she said, handing me a pair of cotton trousers. I looked at her blankly and she laughed. "You've never hemmed a pair of pants?"

"Just show me the basic stitch. I'll get the hang of it." I sounded more confident than I felt.

"Can you thread a needle?" she asked.

"Very funny. Of course I can. Where's the thread?"

She pointed at a clear plastic sewing box that looked reassuringly like a tackle box, and I rummaged through it for needle and thread. The pants were tan, and like a real pro I selected a light-colored thread, feeling inordinately proud of myself. I settled down in a chair and stealthily slipped the thread through the eye of the needle. When I looked up, she was watching me with amusement.

"What?"

"No, nothing. You're doing fine."

"That's what you told Markie. And Pontius Pilate for that matter. And Mary Jane. You're a terrible liar."

"No, really. Here, let me help you get started." She took the needle from me, made a deft little knot at the end and poked the needle through the pant leg pulling the thread behind it in a neat even stitch. I watched her do it three or four times and then took over.

"Ouch!" I said.

She looked up startled, then tried to hide her grin. "You need a thimble?"

"Oh, no. I enjoy pain. Really." I stuck my finger in my mouth and sucked at the pinprick of blood. Then I bent over my task, intent on success.

While I stitched, she sat at the sewing machine and worked magic. The gentle hum accompanied her fluid movements and I couldn't help glancing up to watch her work. Unfortunately, whenever I did, I managed to stick myself. I was getting good at not crying out. I simply wiped the blood away as discreetly as I could and continued working. The hem of the pant leg, however, was dotted here and there with red. I hoped it wouldn't show onstage.

"There!" she declared triumphantly, making me start. Once again, I pricked myself, and this time I let out the teensiest shriek. When I looked up she was laughing.

"Sorry, I didn't mean to startle you." She was holding up a red silky shift, examining her work. "Would you mind being my guinea pig here? I just need to hem this. And it looks like your fingers could use the rest."

"Ha ha," I said.

"Here." She tossed me the red dress. "You can change in the bathroom."

"You want me to put this on?" For some reason, I felt a sudden wave of panic wash over me. I hadn't worn a dress since high school.

"You don't mind, do you? I just need to mark it for hemming. You're about the same height as Mary Jane." She must have seen the look on my face. "I'd put it on and let *you* do the hemming, but I'm afraid I'd need a blood transfusion afterward."

I could still hear her chuckling as I trudged down the hall toward the bathroom.

Women wore dresses all the time, I told myself as I slipped out of my clothes in front of the mirror. So why did I feel like I was about to dress in drag? Of course, I was already in costume, so to speak. What was the difference between wearing teenybopper clothes and this red silky thing? I slipped it over my head and felt it slide down my body.

I felt totally naked. The soft fabric whispered against my skin, raising goose bumps. My nipples had become instantly hard, and I rubbed at them, willing them to calm down. This was ridiculous. Why hadn't I worn a bra? I looked at myself in the mirror and was startled by my reflection. The red dress, which made me feel vulnerable and unprotected, looked sexy as hell. If it had been on someone else, I'd have loved it. As it was, I was paralyzed with fear.

"You okay in there?" Lauren asked, just outside the door.

"Uh, yeah. It's just that I don't think this thing fits right."

"Let me see," she said. The door flew open and we stood facing each other. I felt her gaze slide down my body and heat rushed to my cheeks. I stood my ground, fighting the urge to throw my arms across my chest.

"I'd say that that *thing* fits absolutely perfectly," she said, mimicking my words. But the look in her eyes had changed from humor to something else. For the briefest flicker of a moment, I thought she might have been looking at me with more than professorial interest. But as quickly as it had appeared, the look vanished, and she turned away. Reluctantly, I followed her to the dining room. "This will just take a minute," she said, kneeling in front of me. She had a row of pins between her lips and her words were garbled. Now and then, the backs of her hands brushed against my thighs as she worked, sending disturbing signals up my body. I was glad she was focused on the hemming job, because my nipples had grown quite erect again. I couldn't believe the way my damn body was responding to something as innocent as having someone hem a dress.

But it wasn't just that, I knew. For one thing, I found Dr. Lauren Monroe damned attractive, and for another thing, the dress I was wearing made me feel totally exposed. She was only inches away, touching me, and I could feel her breath on my thighs. It had been a long, long time. I drew in a lengthy sigh and let it out slowly, trying not to shudder.

"There," she said, patting my hip as she got to her feet. "That wasn't so bad, was it?" Obviously, she had no idea.

She stood back and examined her work, and I saw her take in the condition of my nipples. Her eyes met mine and there was an instant of absolute, irrefutable recognition. I could tell it threw her. She stepped backward, tugging at the wisps of blonde hair that curled around her ears.

"You must be cold," she said. "Go ahead and change. Then I'll just finish hemming that." She had already moved back to the table and was digging through the piles of fabric as if she had lost something.

I rushed to the bathroom to change.

"You want another Coke?" she asked, not looking up when I returned. I was much more comfortable, now that I was back in my jeans. I decided to throw caution to the wind.

"I can't handle more than one a day," I said. "Too sweet. I'd take a beer, though."

She glanced up. "Are you old enough?"

So this was it. The moment of truth. Well actually, the moment of deception.

"I'm twenty-five. Why? How old do I look?" I couldn't help it. I really wanted to know.

"To tell the truth, you do seem older than the other students. I haven't seen too many twenty-five-year-olds at Kings Harbor." She looked at me questioningly.

"Well, I kind of took some time off. I've been in Europe." Where this came from, I had no idea. It just flew out of my mouth before I could stop it.

"Really?" She perked up. "Where in Europe? And what were you doing there?" She had walked into the kitchen and was rummaging through the refrigerator. Apparently she'd decided that if I was twenty-five, she'd allow me to drink a beer.

"Paris," I said. "Mostly." As soon as I said it, I knew where the whole thing had come from. I hadn't thought much about Maggie all day, but somehow she had managed to worm her way into the conversation.

"I've always dreamed of going to Paris," she said. "What's it like?" She handed me a bottle of Full Sail Ale. "It's all I have. I hope it's okay. Corey's friend Pete likes them."

"It's fine, thanks." I took a small sip and wondered how I was going to get out of talking about Paris. All I knew was the little Maggie had told me. And frankly, I hadn't been paying all that much attention. "You want me to do these pants like the last ones?" I asked, hoping to change the subject. I noticed she'd poured herself a glass of white wine.

"If your fingers can take the abuse," she said. "What were you doing in Paris?"

"Well, I was just sort of tagging along," I improvised. "My lover was there, uh, working, and I was doing some writing." It was all I could think of. I was digging myself in deeper, but I didn't know how to stop.

"You're a writer?" she said.

"I'm working on it. But I've decided it's time to go back to school, finish my degree and make an honest living. To tell you the truth, it's been quite an adjustment, coming back to the States. The college kids seem so much younger than I remembered. I guess it's because I'm older than when I left."

"That does tend to happen. Where do you plan to go to school in the fall?"

"I've been accepted at UCLA," I said. At least this was common ground. If she asked me something about UCLA I could probably answer.

"That's wonderful. How long were you in Paris?" She obviously wasn't going to let this die a quiet death.

"Well, in Paris, just this last year. Before that, we were

in Spain. My Spanish is a lot better than my French. We didn't do that much socializing the last year." If she asked me to say something in French, I was dead.

"Hmmm." She sipped her wine and resumed stitching the red dress.

I picked up another pair of pants and started hemming. My hands were trembling and sweaty. I didn't like lying like this. But I didn't know how to stop.

"It sounds fascinating," she said at last. "What does your lover do that takes him to Europe?"

"She's a teacher," I said. "She's been teaching English as a Second Language. Actually she still is. I came back alone."

Lauren had quit sewing and was looking at me strangely. She seemed at a loss for words.

"We broke up," I offered.

"I see." Her voice was curt. Her shoulders had stiffened and her whole face seemed to go hard. She started sewing again, but the smooth fluid motions were replaced by short choppy ones. She was clearly upset.

"Did I say something wrong?"

"Of course not," she said. She was sewing furiously now, her rapid movements a blur.

"It's because my lover was a woman, isn't it?" I said. "That bothers you."

"No, of course not."

"But it does. You can't even bring yourself to look at me."

She finally let her eyes meet mine, and they were full of turmoil. She shook her head slowly. "If I've done anything to give you the wrong impression..." she started. "I mean, if I, in any way, gave you the idea that I was interested in you in any way other than a..."

I almost laughed. "Look, professor." I stood up and set the full bottle on the table very carefully. "You didn't give me any impression one way or the other. My being a lesbian has absolutely no bearing on anything to do with you. They assigned me to your class because your T.A. dropped out and I was glad to help, not just because it helps me get a T.A. position at the semester, but because you seemed like someone who could use a hand. Anything else you've read into my behavior is your imagination."

Which was a lie, I knew. I *had* been attracted to her. Before I discovered she was such a homophobic prude.

Heart pounding, face burning, I grabbed my shoes and stormed out the door without bothering to put them on. I heard her call my name from the doorway but I didn't even slow down. By the time I got to my apartment, I was almost out of breath.

Chapter Ten

I paced the tiny living room, fuming. Words, much
more brilliant than any I'd used, poured out, my mind
reeling. How could I have been so stupid! I couldn't believe
that for one second I'd considered her attractive. Obviously,
I hadn't seen beyond the shallow good looks. Just because
she had a gay brother, I'd assumed, at the very least, she'd
be open.

And why had I even thrown in the part about a female
lover? I asked myself, pacing. Because I'd wanted her to
know. I was testing the waters. I just hadn't expected such
a conservative response. Well, I'd gotten what I deserved.
It served me right. What business did I have coming on to

a straight woman, anyway? I was supposed to be working a case. I grabbed my jacket, slammed the door and headed out to find a pay phone from which to call Martha.

"Sherlock," Martha crooned, "I wondered when I'd hear from you. You all settled in?"

"Yeah. It's a good thing I didn't bring more than one suitcase. I don't know where I'd have put it."

She chuckled. "You don't sound too happy. Any luck so far?"

"Well, the roommate of the deceased wants me to move in with her. I'd like to get a chance to peek through Lisa's stuff before the sister comes to take it away, and I also think Lisa might've kept a diary. If she did, I'd love to get my hands on it. No one seems to think she killed herself, but they're not thinking murder either. Apparently she dabbled in recreational drugs, so it's possible she just decided to take a midnight swim and passed out. I don't know. I'm hoping to find out more tomorrow."

"Are they buying your cover?"

"So far. I got a little carried away over at the drama professor's house. I told her I'd spent the last few years in Europe. If she asks me to *parlez vous Francais,* I'm up a creek."

"You were at the professor's house? How'd you manage that?"

"She needed help sewing costumes. I am her assistant, after all. I thought I might get some information." I realized somewhat belatedly that I hadn't even pumped the professor for information. I'd been too busy wondering about her personal life.

"Why is it I get the feeling there's more to this than you're telling me?"

"Because you thrive on intrigue. And you have an overactive imagination."

"Don't tell me. This professor just happens to be cute. Am I right?"

"Martha, don't be ridiculous. She's a homophobic

prude. You should have seen her reaction when she found out I was gay."

"And just exactly how did she find *that* out? I thought you were undercover." Martha's voice held more humor than anything else, but I felt like a fool.

"Jake always said to stick as close to the truth as possible," I said, embarrassed. "And besides, for a fleeting moment, I thought she might be one of us. I guess I don't have your knack for foolproof lesbian detection. But you'd think with her brother dying of AIDS and all, she'd be a little less judgmental."

"My, you did get personal. Any moles I should be aware of? Did you get her brand of deodorant?"

"Cute, Martha."

"Well at least you won't be wasting your time with her now. Maybe you'll be able to concentrate on the case." She was right and I knew it. Martha had a way of cutting through the bull and getting to the heart of a matter. I silently vowed to put my anger at the professor behind me and get on with my investigation.

"Speaking of investigations, I've been thinking about your serial killer," I said.

"Good. I could use a fresh point of view. But I do wish you'd quit referring to him as mine."

I ignored this. "Six months ago, Sarah Ringer was this guy's first victim, right?"

"As far as we know."

"And that was right here in Kings Harbor. Then, four months later the second victim, Tracy Lee, was found a hundred miles south of here in Gold Beach. Then, only two months later, your third victim was found about a hundred miles north of here in Lincoln City. It seems to me, this guy is not only picking up his pace, but that he's working inside a two-hundred-mile radius, with Kings Harbor in the center. I think this might be his home base."

"Maybe, Cass. But it could also be that he's someone

who makes his living driving up and down the coast. A delivery man, a logger, a salesman. That's why the terrible twins, as I've taken to calling them, are concentrating their efforts in Lincoln City. They're checking motel records and matching them against the registers of those in Gold Beach and Kings Harbor on the nights of the first two murders. Who knows? Maybe they'll come up with something, but somehow, I don't think so. Like this guy is going to use his real name? Come on. Even if he did stay in motels, which I doubt, he'd use cash, right? Besides, we got a partial tire print at the last scene, which may or may not belong to the perp's vehicle. If it does, then our best guess is the guy drives some kind of pickup, van or sports utility vehicle. The rain screwed up the tread marks but at least the width of the tire indicates a larger vehicle. If he's got four-wheel drive, he could be taking them almost anywhere to do his dirty work."

"Gee, Martha. That narrows it down. You just described half of the vehicles in Oregon. Even I've got four-wheel drive."

"I know, babe. And we don't know for sure the tracks are even his. Anyway, with the Feds up in Lincoln City, it's been nice and peaceful here. While they've been scouring motels and local flower shops in that area, I decided to check out the florists around here."

"Why florists?"

"Sally Thompson had a red rose petal clutched in her palm, and we think the perp might have brought her roses. Anyway, I found a guy at the Flower Barrel right here in Kings Harbor that remembers selling a dozen red roses to a young man the night before Thanksgiving. Most of the orders are for mixed bouquets, or those cornucopia things, so he remembers the order because it was unusual. Unfortunately, that's about all he remembers. No hair color, no height, nothing. Just the impression that it was a young guy. Of course, this guy's pushing eighty, so anyone might seem young. Still, it's a start." She paused. "You are right about one thing, though. This asshole is definitely picking up his pace. Not exactly a warming thought, considering our lack of progress. It's like he leaves us evidence on purpose, but so little of it is useful. I mean, the guy goes to all the trouble of cleaning his victims, and then he leaves us the condoms? It doesn't make sense."

"What do you mean, he cleans them?"

"All three women had their bodies scoured, especially their pubic regions. No stray pubic hairs, no skin under their nails, nothing. He must wear gloves. Even the bite marks aren't much help unless we find the creep and can match the marks with his teeth. He pours ammonia in the bite wounds, erasing any evidence of saliva. He's a smart bastard, Cass. And he's very careful. He only leaves us what he wants us to find."

We let the silence hang between us. Finally, Martha changed the subject. "Have you heard from Maggie?"

"I haven't checked," I said.

"Well, that's progress!" She laughed. "That brooding, desperate phase you've been going through just isn't you. So, besides the disappointingly straight college prof, have you met anyone interesting?"

"Martha, I've been here two days," I said, exasperated. "And I'm on a case. I didn't come looking for a fling with a college kid. Has it occurred to you that ever since you've embarked on your very first monogamous relationship, you spend an inordinate amount of time living vicariously through what you wish was my adventurous love life? I hate to keep disappointing you, but I'm just not you!"

She laughed again, her rich deep voice making it impossible for me not to smile too. "Keep practicing, kiddo. You'll get the hang of it." She hung up and left me grinning.

She might be right, I thought. If nothing else, at least my mild, fleeting interest in the professor had helped quell the burning loneliness that Maggie's departure created. For the first time in months, there was a bit of bounce in my step. Even my anger at the professor was preferable to wallowing in self-pity. Martha was absolutely right. Brooding wasn't my thing.

I was about to leave the booth and head back to Mama Mangione's for a repeat performance of last night's Early-Bird Special when I felt a tap on my shoulder. I whirled around and found myself looking up at Markie Lewis. He was dressed in faded Levi's with the knees artfully torn and a white turtleneck sweater tucked into the low-riding jeans. His head was cocked to one side and he had a lazy, lopsided grin I was sure he practiced in the mirror.

"You're the new T.A.," he stated, his gaze casually roving my body. I resisted an involuntary urge to cringe.

"You're Judas," I said, hoping my smile looked genuine.

"So, what'd you think?"

"About the play?"

He nodded, crossing his arms in what I felt sure was an effort to show off his biceps. He leaned against the telephone booth in a well-practiced stance of cool nonchalance. For my comfort, he was standing half-a-foot too close.

"It was pretty good," I said. "Some of the actors seem better than others."

"Oh yeah? Like who?" His dark eyes gleamed, and he ran his fingers through the shock of wavy black hair that graced his forehead. I realized he was flirting with me.

"Well, I thought Jesus was pretty good," I said, knowing this would drive him crazy.

"Brad? Shit, he can't hardly carry a note half the time!"

"Well, he's kind of cute, though. And he makes a good Jesus."

"I guess."

"And I thought Pontius Pilate was believable. I loved his voice."

"No way! Roland Pipps is the biggest fag on campus! He sings like a girl. You really thought he was good?"

"I said he was believable. Although I guess he did sort of cut people's lines off."

"Have you ever heard him talk?" Markie asked. "I mean when he's not reciting lines? He stu-stu-stutters li-li-like th-th-this." He laughed cruelly at his own imitation.

"I hadn't noticed."

"That's because he won't hardly talk in front of anyone. I wouldn't either if I was him. So, what else did you think?" He was fishing for compliments so shamelessly I was tempted to go on torturing his ego, but for the sake of the investigation, I gave him what he wanted.

"I thought you had the best voice of the lot."

"No way. Really? The best?"

"Definitely. You make a very compelling Judas."

"Like, what do you mean exactly. By compelling, I mean." He either didn't know what the word meant, or he wanted me to go on and on. Probably the latter.

"I mean, when you were onstage, it was like the rest of the characters faded into the background. All eyes automatically seem to go to you. It's obvious you're a natural. Of course, I'm no expert or anything."

"No, no. You seem real knowledgeable. I appreciate your honesty. Can I ask you something personal?"

"Sure," I said. This guy was so full of himself, I doubted his personal question would be about me at all. I was right.

"Did you think I was singing too loud at first? I mean, Dr. Monroe told me to tone things down, but I think that was just her way of getting me to go along with Professor Pervert so there wouldn't be a scene. Don't you think she was just being polite?"

Oh, how I longed to tell him the truth. I bit my tongue. "It could be that the orchestra just wasn't playing loud enough," I offered. "Professor Pervert?"

He threw back his handsome head and laughed. "We just call him that behind his back. His real name's Purvis. But he's an asshole. You know, I think maybe you're right. They should be playing louder, rather than me singing lower. Will you mention that to Dr. Monroe?"

"I could suggest it, I guess. But she's the director. Hey, aren't you the one who used to date that girl who drowned?"

"Who told you that?" His dark eyes narrowed and he recrossed his arms.

"I just heard everyone talking about it. I mean, the whole campus is upset over what happened. I've just heard bits and pieces, though. I don't remember who mentioned that you were her boyfriend."

"Well, whoever it was had it wrong. Sure, we dated. But it's not like we were an item. I date lots of girls." He gave me a long, meaningful look.

"Still, it must have been hard on you. Being with her that night, and then her turning up dead the next day. It must have been a real shock."

"I never said it wasn't upsetting. Jeez, whaddaya think? It's not like I'm insensitive. I just resent everyone's lumping us together. The other day someone asked if we were engaged!" He let out a snort of laughter.

"What do you think happened?" I asked, pushing my luck. It was a lot harder getting information when you couldn't just come out and say you were investigating a case.

He narrowed his eyes at me again. "Shit, how am I supposed to know? She was stoned. She was drunk. Last I saw of her, she could barely walk. If I'da known she was gonna go for a swim, I'd have stopped her. But she didn't say nothing about it. I was off with Brad and them, anyway. I figured she got a ride home with someone else. I don't think anyone will ever know why she decided to go in the water. She just did, that's all. It was a senseless tragedy and nothing we can say or do can change it."

He looked down and rubbed his eyes with the back of a knuckle. I think he wanted me to believe he was wiping tears, and if his last line hadn't sounded like something he'd rehearsed, I might have fallen for it. He was doing a better job of acting now than he had onstage.

"Do you think she might have done it on purpose?" I asked.

He shrugged, keeping his eyes down while he continued to wipe at imaginary tears and shook his head. I was getting the full treatment.

"I'm sorry. I didn't mean to upset you."

"That's okay," he said, taking one last knuckle-swipe across his eyes. He'd rubbed his skin pink, which added to the illusion that he'd been crying. "Sometimes I just get tired of talking about it. I just need to get on with life, you know? I can't go on day after day feeling so sad. That's why we're going back to the dunes Wednesday night. Kind of our way of saying life goes on, you know?"

"You mean, back to where it happened?" For some reason, this made the little hairs on the back of my neck stand straight up.

"Well, just to the general area. It's kind of a hangout. You should come. The dunes are awesome. You can sit up there and watch the waves crashing below. We usually build a fire, drink some beers, just kick it, you know? Sometimes guys bring their dune buggies, and sometimes we just sit and listen to some tunes. Wednesday, I know everyone will be thinking about Lisa. It'll be good to talk about it, get it out of our systems, so to speak. No one felt like going last weekend."

"Sounds fun," I said lamely. The best I could tell, Markie was asking me out on a date. The mere idea nauseated me, but there was no way I was going to pass

70

up an opportunity to visit the scene of the crime, if indeed a crime had even been committed.

"All right, then," he said, as if it had all been decided. "If you want, I could pick you up. My truck's got four-wheel drive."

Now my neck hairs were really standing, but I managed to arch an eyebrow in question.

"The sand," he explained. "It's a pain if you have to walk the whole way up. I like to drive as far as I can. So what's your address? I'll come get you before five. This time of year, it gets dark early."

Markie was apparently unaccustomed to being turned down. I didn't disappoint him. I gave him my address.

"Cool. I guess I'll see you at rehearsal tomorrow, right?"

"I can hardly wait," I said. Only the promise of Mama Mangioni's manicotti enabled me to overcome another bout of nausea. I didn't know whose performance sickened me more, though, his or mine.

Chapter Eleven

The second night on a strange mattress is always worse than the first. I couldn't get comfortable and my mind was as restless as my body. When I finally dosed off, my subconscious played a cruel trick.

Maggie was radiant. Her black curly hair was plastered to her brow with sweat and her dark eyes smouldered with passion. She hovered above me, a teasing grin on her lips. I arched up, trying to reach her, but she pulled back and I awoke with a start.

I cursed. I sighed. I rolled over, buried my head in the pillow and tried desperately to make the dream come back.

I ignored the single tear that had seeped out and trickled into my ear.

The dream had completely ruined whatever chance I'd had of a good night's sleep. At four in the morning, I got up. It was still dark outside, but the nearly full moon had begun to penetrate a thick cloud cover, lending the sky an eerie, surreal quality. Maybe the sky was always eerie at four in the morning, I thought, shrugging into my jacket.

I pretended not to know where I was going, but of course I did. Any private eye worth her salt would have been drawing up plans or spying on a suspect or something. But, despite a big show of appreciating the pre-dawn splendor, I headed straight for the phone booth I'd used earlier that day and called my own number.

There were three messages, and none of them was from Maggie.

"Face it, Cassidy," I said to myself. "She's left you. You know it, she knows it, and everyone you know knows it." I started walking east down Elm Street, almost enjoying the cold damp air. When you're miserable, unpleasant things seem welcome.

A funny thing happened as I walked. I found it wasn't Maggie I was missing so much as my cats, Gammon and Panic. After all, they'd been the ones who had comforted me when Maggie left. They'd been with me since the death of Diane. From the moment Martha had brought them to me as a housewarming gift, they'd been a major part of my life. Two tiny balls of fur had turned into gorgeous, fun-loving companions.

They bird-dogged me when it suited them, following me down to the dock, leaping into the boat for a joy ride or sprawling on the dock in the sun while I worked on my boat. Sometimes they fought, battling for Top Cat status. Just as often they curled up next to each other, basking in the shared warmth.

They chased and caught every crawling, slithering, flying beast known to man.

They swatted my ankles, bit my hair, purred into my ear and kneaded my thighs. When I was feeling down, they pressed themselves into my body and wouldn't budge.

I realized with a pang that made me stop walking and look up at the thinly veiled moon that my cats would never, ever leave me. Lovers would. Lovers had. But Panic and Gammon, at least until death did us part, would never pick up and traipse off to Paris. Let alone to Switzerland. I was pretty sure.

I let my gaze slide from the muzzled yellow orb of the moon to the complex in front of me. Had I meant to come here? The fence around Lisa Lane's lawn stood out in the early morning light like white sharks' teeth. Ominous. It seemed to fit my mood.

Suddenly, the lights inside her townhouse came on. I stood transfixed, wondering if somehow Rhonda had seen me standing beneath her window, staring up at it. Then, before I could slink back into the darkness, I heard a muffled thump, like a sack of mud falling to the ground. The hairs on my arms stood up and my chest tightened.

The noise had come from around the building toward the back. I edged toward the sound, trying to ignore my rapid pulse. The moon was playing tricks with my eyes and the breeze rustled leaves so that every sound made me flinch. It was probably just a cat, I told myself. Or a raccoon. I strained to see through the darkness, my body taut with apprehension.

Suddenly, something moved. There, crouched below Lisa Lane's bedroom window, was a dark shape. No sooner had I seen it than it sprang up and dashed into the alley beside the building, disappearing into the night. I started to give chase, but a loud shriek stopped me before I even reached the alley. I looked up and saw Rhonda's silhouette in the open window above. She had her hand to her mouth, like some silent film star, stifling a silent scream. I rushed to her front door and pressed the doorbell.

"Rhonda, it's me. Cassidy James! I saw someone climb out the window just now. Are you okay?" I had to repeat this several times.

"Cassidy? What are you doing here?" Her voice was tiny, scared.

"I couldn't sleep. I was just walking around. I think I interrupted a burglary. Can I come in?"

Slowly, the door opened a crack. Rhonda's brown eyes peered out at me, her brow furrowed. She looked above me, behind me. Finally, she opened the door wide enough for me to enter. As soon as I did, she slammed the door and locked it behind us.

"Someone was in the house!" she said, her eyes registering the full extent of her fear. "I heard them. When I turned on the light, whoever it was must've climbed back out the window. Look!"

She was clad in a checkered flannel nightgown and worn, fluffy slippers. I followed her ample form down the hallway, past her bedroom and into Lisa's. The room had been trashed.

"You slept through *this*?" Books were scattered across the floor, drawers were turned upside down on the bed and clothes lay piled in a heap in the center of the room. It was my turn to look bewildered.

"I'm a heavy sleeper," she said, looking apologetic. "And he must've been awfully quiet. The sound I heard was like a little scraping noise. He must've taken his time. Otherwise, I'm sure I would've heard him."

"Do you see anything missing?" I watched as she made a half-hearted attempt at poking through the rubble and then shook her head. Once again, I felt she was hiding something. "Why do you think someone would break into Lisa's room in the middle of the night and go through her stuff?"

I watched her closely. Her eyes slid to the left before meeting mine. I wasn't sure why, but Rhonda Lou was lying to me just as she had when I'd asked about Lisa's diary.

"I have no idea," she said. "Maybe someone wanted something, you know, like something they had lent her, but were too embarrassed just to ask me for it. Did you get a good look at who it was?"

"I'm not even sure if they were male or female," I said truthfully. "Although from the size, I'm assuming male. He was dressed in dark clothing, and I only saw him running away. But I don't think he had anything with him. I mean, I don't think he found what he was looking for. What do you think it could have been?"

Rhonda glanced to the right this time before assuming wide-eyed wonder, and she shrugged as if the whole thing were beyond her. She was obviously hiding something. She knew, or thought she knew, what they'd come for, but she wasn't about to tell me.

I went to the window and examined the lock. The intruder wouldn't have had to be an expert to break in, I thought. The little spring-loaded latch was a cinch, once the window was lifted up a quarter of an inch. I showed Rhonda how easy it was and then re-locked the window.

"I guess I'll ask the landlord to put on new locks," she said. "Come on, let's get out of here. This room is giving me the creeps."

I followed her into the living room. By now, all the lights were ablaze. It was hard to believe it was just past five in the morning.

"You want some coffee?"

I nodded, walking around the living room, wondering if I should reveal my identity. Maybe if I did, she'd tell me what it was she was hiding. On the other hand, she might just put up more barriers. And I was beginning to think I knew what it was. I had convinced myself that Rhonda not only knew that Lisa kept a diary but also knew exactly where it was. And I had a feeling someone else wanted to get to it first. Which is exactly what I wanted, too. If Rhonda knew I was onto her, she might get rid of it before I could find it. I'd have to come back later, when she wasn't here, and do my own little search. Not of Lisa's room, but of Rhonda's.

"You take cream or sugar?"

"Just black."

She handed me an earthenware mug and curled up on the sofa with her own steaming cup between her palms. Her face still bore the marks of heavy sleep.

"I still can't believe you were just happening by. What were you doing out in the middle of the night?"

"Like I said, I was having trouble sleeping. I thought a walk might help. I just sort of ended up here. Maybe it was fate. Hey, shouldn't we call the police?" It was the last thing I wanted her to do, but it would have been strange not to suggest it. Frankly, I was surprised she hadn't already called.

"I don't see what good it would do. I mean, nothing was stolen. I'm betting it was just one of Lisa's friends, you know, wanting something that belonged to them. Anyway, her stuff will all be gone this week. Her sister's coming to get it on Thursday. And I'll get those locks changed right away. I hope this doesn't change your mind about moving in. It's the first time anything like this has happened. Honest. It's really a very safe neighborhood." She was babbling now, steering me away from her deception, and I let her.

"I've got to be going," I said at last. "I've got an early class, and I need to shower. How about you? What time are your classes?"

"Not until ten. I like to sleep in." She giggled at the absurdity of this, seeing as how it was still dark outside.

"When will you know about rooming together?" she asked, walking me to the door. Now that I was leaving, she seemed hesitant to let me go. I couldn't blame her, considering what had happened.

"I'll let you know soon," I promised. I stepped back into the pre-dawn chill and hugged my jacket around me. I'd be back before she knew it, I thought. In fact, if I could sneak away from my T.A. duties, I'd be back shortly past ten.

I walked until the early-morning sun peeked through the trees to the east. I thought about Maggie's leaving me, about Lisa Lane's death, about Rhonda's probable lie and about the professor's reaction to my gayness. I also thought about the three women someone had mutilated and killed. What would make someone do such a thing? What kind of sickness would drive someone to such horror? I was almost certain that the serial killings were unrelated to the death of Lisa Lane, but I wasn't positive that Lisa's death was as innocent as everyone thought. Martha's doubts had finally begun to worm their way into my own suspicious mind.

The weak sun was no match for the steely clouds crowding in from the ocean and I shivered all the way to the drama building.

To my relief, the door was unlocked. Might as well get some painting done before anyone else arrived, I thought. The truth was, I just didn't want to come face to face with the professor. With any luck, I could finish before she even got there. Which was silly thinking on my part, I knew. If I was going to continue playing the role of her T.A., I'd have to interact with her eventually.

I slipped inside and made my way through the darkish interior, not wanting to turn on the lights. When at last I found the prop room, I felt my way to the little side room where we'd seen the unpainted flats. I didn't turn on the lights until I was safely inside.

Half-expecting something sinister after Rhonda's break-in, I was almost disappointed when I found only the blank flats awaiting me. With a sigh, I rummaged through the cupboards for the right supplies, and before I knew it, I was diligently rolling black paint over the canvas partitions.

It was very therapeutic. I rolled away my frustrations, swiped at my anger, rubbed out my hurt. I was literally on a roll. I may have been setting a world record.

I didn't notice the light outside changing. The one window was off to the side toward my back. I didn't even think about the time. When I heard the cry from the other side of the wall, it took me completely by surprise.

Something crashed down, and then someone swore. But they didn't sound mad. They sounded scared.

Without thinking, I rushed out of my oblong enclosure and dashed into the prop room. The room was dark and silent. I stood still, listening, peering into the darkness. Then I heard it again. Somewhere down the hall.

On tiptoe, I worked my way through the dark. I knew by now it was light outside, but in here, where no windows let in the light, it was still as dark as midnight. I would have turned on a light if I'd known where a switch was. As it was, I groped my way forward, using the walls to guide me.

"Help," the voice called again. No hysteria. Just plain fear.

"Hello?" I said, opening closet doors.

"In here," the voice cried, sounding stronger. Across the hallway, a sliver of light was creeping out from beneath a door. I raced across the hallway and flung open the door.

"Lauren?"

She was standing high up on a ladder, clutching the top rung with white fists. A cardboard box was wedged between her forehead and the ladder. Two boxes lay at the foot of the ladder, their contents sprawled across the floor.

"Cassidy?" she asked, her voice trembling.

"What's wrong?" I was looking desperately around the tiny room for villains. I'd expected the worst. It didn't take me long, however, to realize that no one else was in the room.

"I can't get down," she said.

"Are you hurt?"

There was no answer. Just a long, heavy sigh. "I'm afraid," she said, finally.

"Of what?"

"Heights."

"Oh." It wasn't brilliant, but what else could I say?

"I've been up here a long time," she offered.

"Okay," I said, finally making my mind work. The truth was, part of me wanted to laugh. I mean, this was the woman who'd practically kicked me out of her apartment because I was gay. It would serve her right if I just left her up there to panic. But she was obviously suffering. "It's okay," I said. "Just let go of the box and I'll catch it."

"It's breakable."

"Don't worry, Professor. I'm right here. Even if you fell right now, I'd catch you. Understand? What I want you to do is hold the box above your head, lean into the ladder and move your right leg down one rung."

This was met with utter silence.

"Professor?"

"I liked it better when you called me Lauren." Her voice was that of an obstinate child.

"Okay, Lauren. Now you just do as I say and you'll be down in no time. Ready? Lift the box, lean into the ladder,

lift your right foot and step down onto the next rung.
Lauren? You have to move your foot."

Slowly, like someone stepping onto the moon for the
first time, she lowered her right foot. When at last it hit
the rung, I nearly cheered.

"That's it!"

"Am I almost down?"

"You're getting there," I said cheerily. She was going to
owe me big-time for this one. I didn't even like her.

"Okay, Lauren. Now, you're going to move your left
foot to the same spot. Piece of cake, right? Just pick it up
and move it down."

"Cassidy?"

"I'm right here."

"You probably think this is ridiculous, don't you?'

Actually, I did. "Of course not. We all have fears."

"Not you, probably." She was stalling and I knew it.
She was afraid to move her foot down.

"Tell you what. You move your left foot down to the
next rung and maybe I'll tell you what my greatest fear
is."

She considered this for about an hour. Finally, she took
a huge gulp and haltingly lowered her left leg. "There!"
she cried. Her arms were shaking, still holding the
cardboard box.

"What's in that thing, anyway?"

"Don't change the subject. What's your greatest fear?"

Jeez! I couldn't believe this. Here I was doing a good
deed for a woman who'd insulted me, and now she was
demanding secrets. What could I say? That my greatest
fear was that I'd continue falling for women who wouldn't
love me in return? That if they did love me, they'd die on
me, like Diane had, or leave me like Maggie?

"The sooner you get down, the better you'll feel. Come
on, just take one step at a time."

Lauren must have heard something in my voice, because she quit arguing and took two shaky steps down the ladder.

"I'd feel better if I just knew your hands were up there. I know it's stupid, okay? Just humor me."

I stretched as far as I could reach and she took another tentative step until my hands brushed the backs of her thighs. The longer she stalled, the more uncomfortable I became. Her thighs were firm and warm and I could feel a faint trembling through the thin layer of cotton.

Cautiously, she lowered her left foot and then, a century later, her right foot followed. By then, both of my hands cupped her buttocks. I started to pull away but she pressed against me.

"Don't you dare move!" she ordered.

I stifled the urge to laugh. This was great. The woman who less than twenty-four hours ago had cringed in disgust at my lesbianism was now begging me to keep my hands on her rear end. Damn her, anyway. Why couldn't she just hurry this up? But Lauren seemed relieved to feel the pressure of my hands and she leaned into them. Before I knew what was happening, we were both tumbling backwards.

Like with so many things that happen suddenly, time seemed to stretch out into slow motion. I knew we were falling but could do nothing to break the fall. Both of my arms were wrapped around Lauren, who somehow managed to hang onto the box.

I heard my head hit the wall behind us and felt Lauren's head slam into my lip. I worked to keep my feet beneath me but felt them buckle as I slumped to the floor. I cushioned Lauren's fall, and she landed in a heap on my lap. Somehow, during the fall, my hands had risen up to cup her breasts.

Suddenly, time slipped back into reality, and Lauren was struggling to her feet. I couldn't tell if she was crying or giggling.

"Are you okay?" she asked. She stood above me, still clutching the box in her hands.

"God, I'm sorry," I muttered, my face on fire. I was mortified for having touched her that way.

"It's not your fault. I shouldn't have leaned back so far. Oh, you're bleeding." Apparently, she had chosen to ignore my unintentional fondling. She finally set the box down and leaned over to examine my lip. She reached into a pocket and pulled out a tissue, which she used to dab at my lower lip. Just that fast, she'd gone from terrified and helpless to maternal. I pushed myself off the floor, still embarrassed. "I suppose you think I'm an absolute idiot," she said.

"Not at all." I dabbed at the blood with the tissue. "Like I said, we all have fears. But maybe you should have someone else get the high stuff from now on."

"I wasn't talking about that," she said. We were standing just a few feet apart, and I could see the blue of her eyes deepen. "I meant yesterday. I'm really sorry about what happened. It wasn't at all how it seemed. I just — it's just that you took me by surprise. I'd like to make it up to you."

"Not necessary," I said. "I've learned to respect other people's phobias. It's like fear of heights, I guess. Homophobia must be just as scary as anything else."

"You're not listening," she said, her eyes flashing. "Look, I can't blame you for being mad, but I'd like a chance to explain. And I can't do it here. Maybe you'd agree to have dinner with me tomorrow tonight? Give me a chance?"

My heart was thudding ridiculously, and I feared it showed on my face. Had this woman just asked me out on a date? Of course not, I told myself. She was just feeling guilty about her reaction to my gayness. She didn't want me to think she was a bigot, that was all. I tried to shrug nonchalantly.

"Well, I appreciate the gesture, Lauren, but the truth

is, I've already got plans for Wednesday night. Some other time, maybe?" My voice was cool and remote, just the way I wanted it. There was no way I wanted her to know that my stomach was fluttering.

Her reaction surprised me. Her cheeks darkened, and she began fussing with the strands of hair that had worked their way loose during the fall. She averted her gaze and finally bent over to gather the fallen boxes and their contents.

"Sure," she said. "Some other time will be fine."

I let myself out of the tiny closet and made my way through the dark halls to the storage room where I'd been painting.

I *am* on a case, I kept telling myself. I have a game plan. I'm going to break into Rhonda's apartment and see if I can get my hands on what I hope and pray is Lisa Lane's diary. Then I'll go with Markie tomorrow night and see if I can find out what really happened the night Lisa died.

I also needed to find out more about Sarah Ringer, the first murder victim, and see what else she had in common with Lisa Lane, besides taking a drama class. And then, unless something came up, I could tell Martha that her college connection was a dead-end. I would not, under any circumstances, allow myself to become involved with a straight woman. I would not even think about her again.

By the time I finished painting the flats, the rehearsal was in full swing. As I was making my escape, I heard voices backstage and stopped to listen. I stood in the shadows and felt like a voyeur as I watched Rita Colby, the wild-haired woman I'd first met yesterday, talking to Pontius Pilate.

"You shouldn't let him get to you, Roland. He's just another prick." Rita's dark eyes sparked in the darkened room.

"He-he bothers me. He called me a fa-fa-fag. I hate

that." Roland's round face was flushed and his brown eyes looked to Rita for understanding. She put her arm around his shoulders and pulled him close.

"Brad Capers doesn't deserve to be in the same room with you, and don't you forget it. You're worth two dozen Brad Capers. Okay? So just shine him on. Besides, the jerk couldn't carry a note if his life depended on it. I heard Mr. Purvis say yours was the only voice in the whole cast he'd pay money to hear."

"He did? You heard him?" Roland's eyes widened with genuine pleasure.

"Hey, hey, hey, Ro-Ro-land, you trying to duh-duh-date Ruh-Ruh-Ruh Rita here?" I looked up to see Brad Capers saunter backstage, looking resplendent in his white robes and sandals, his blond hair tied back in a leather thong. Roland pulled back from Rita's embrace and his face went bright red. Before he could get a single word out, Rita spoke up.

"Hey, Brad, did you hear the news this morning? About that lady who just gave birth to a baby that was half-male, half-female?"

"No way. Really? Whoa. You're joking, right?"

"No, really," Rita said. "She did. The baby had both a penis and a brain."

Brad's mouth dropped open for a split-second, and then a look of pure hatred crossed his otherwise handsome face. His blue eyes became nearly purple slits.

"Very funny, Colby. No wonder you prefer Roly-Poly's company. You've obviously got a thing against real men." He grabbed his crotch and gave it a quick jerking motion, then turned on his heel and strode across the room.

Roland was grinning like a fool. "G-good one, Rita," he said, beaming.

I felt like applauding, but instead I slipped back down the hallway and made it to the side door.

I let myself out into the bright daylight, blinking at

the harshness. I was famished. Mama Mangione's manicotti had long worn off. But one thing I needed more than food was a shower.

I headed for the tiny apartment, sorting out my thoughts on how to proceed, doing my best to ignore the mounting fear that I was allowing myself to fall for someone again.

Chapter Twelve

The memories were beginning to monopolize his every waking hour but he needed them. It was like a quick fix. He knew he'd need more than memories soon, but for now he closed his eyes and hoped no one was beginning to notice how often he seemed to space out. He didn't care, though. Right now, he needed Sally Thompson. He willed her image to materialize and let the scene unfold, allowing him to relish every detail.

* * * * *

As he had hoped, she screamed. Not that it would do her any good. He'd parked the van in a deserted field and there was no one around for miles. Anyway, he knew it wasn't the knife that made them scream like this. It was the way he smiled at them.

He bent forward and gently licked her face. First the left cheek, then the right. She tasted of salt and fear. No blood yet, just sweat and tears. She struggled against the nylon rope to no avail. He licked her chin, letting the tip of his long tongue curl underneath toward the soft flesh of her throat.

When she screamed again, as he knew she would, he clamped his hand over her mouth, leaned forward and calmly bit off the lower lobe of her left ear. Her eyes widened horribly, but soon all attempts to scream ceased completely.

He rarely bothered to gag them anymore. It wasn't necessary.

He chewed the tiny morsel of flesh slowly, ignoring the trickle of blood that dribbled down his chin. His eyes were locked with hers so he knew she was watching. The way they all did.

He swallowed the severed earlobe and smiled. He felt his heart swell with something he thought must be close to love.

Chapter Thirteen

I rang the doorbell three times, just to make sure Rhonda hadn't decided to skip class. I waited for a woman in a turquoise warmup suit to jog by, then, double-checking to make sure no one could see me, I reached into my jacket pocket and extracted my lock picks. Next to my cats, my lock picks were my most prized possession.

The flimsy lock clicked open without any fuss and a moment later I was inside. If she came home now, I could always say the door was unlocked and I'd let myself in to wait. And if she believed that, there was some swampland at the end of Rainbow Lake I could probably sell her.

I made my way straight for Rhonda's room,

experiencing the familiar thud in my chest that breaking and entering always seemed to inspire. Perhaps I'd been a burglar in a past life, I thought. Or maybe there's a little larceny in all our hearts. Still, it worried me, the thrill of fear that surged through me as I tiptoed into Rhonda's room.

You can learn a lot about a person just by looking at her bedroom. Rhonda's was a comfortable mess. Her bed wasn't exactly made, but the spread was pulled up over the covers and across the pillow. She had an old tattered teddy bear propped up on the pillow, and I bet she slept with it at night. Unlike Lisa's closet, Rhonda's was sparsely filled. But that could have been because a great many of her clothes were scattered about the room, piled onto chairs and draped across their backs. The walls of the room were adorned with surprisingly good photographs, and when I saw the fancy Nikon camera on her dresser, it dawned on me that she'd been far too modest about her photographic skills.

The photos, mostly candid closeups, caught expressions I doubted the subjects would have liked. One was of a professor in front of his class, pointing an accusatory finger toward the lens. His lip was curling upward in a snarl. Another showed a group of teenaged boys sunning themselves on a bench. The arrogance she'd caught was powerful. Three boys, so taken with themselves and their good looks that they were oblivious to her camera, as well as to the woman behind it.

Reluctantly, I tore myself away from the photos. Rhonda Lou was one hell of a photographer. I wondered if she realized it.

I was careful not to disturb her belongings as I methodically conducted my search. If I was right about Rhonda's having Lisa's diary, I figured it was somewhere in her room. But where? And why had she taken it in the first place? Was there something in it that Rhonda didn't want others to find? After fifteen minutes of fruitless search, I started to doubt my theory.

It wasn't under her bed or beneath her pillow. It wasn't between the mattresses. Not in her underwear drawer or any other drawer, for that matter, and there were no false bottoms anywhere. It wasn't on her book-shelf or in her clothes hamper. It was not hidden beneath the piles of clothing or tucked away on the top shelf of the closet. I searched the bathroom, the kitchen and the darkroom, all to no avail. I returned to her bedroom and sat on the bed, scanning the room.

Come on, Rhonda. I know you have it. Where is it? I leaned back against her pillow and stared at the ceiling, thinking. Could she have taken it with her? I picked up her teddy bear and tossed it in the air, catching it a few inches from my face. I tossed it again. Then I sat up, grinning.

Along the back seam of the bear was a zipper. I worked it open and found not one but two small diaries tucked safely inside. One was red and had large loopy handwriting. It only took me a moment to confirm that it was Lisa Lane's. The other, a tan leather book, belonged to Rhonda. Her writing was small and precise. I felt my heart skip, as it always did when I was about to do something I shouldn't.

I slipped both books inside my jacket pocket, next to my lock picks, re-zipped the bear's back after stuffing a few of Rhonda's socks inside, and let myself out of the apartment. There was no question Rhonda would soon know that they'd been taken. And I felt terrible for invading her privacy this way — I really did. There were aspects of being a private eye that made me feel like a creep. But it couldn't be helped. I needed to know whatever it was that Rhonda hadn't wanted anyone else to know about Lisa Lane. For Martha's sake, I told myself. So she could get on with her investigation.

It was cold in the tiny apartment, even for the first of December, and the heater didn't do much to help. Outside, clouds had started to shoulder their way across the dunes and seemed to be huddled right over the apartment. I made some instant coffee and curled up on the minuscule love seat with my bag of M&M's and the diaries. I didn't know exactly what I was looking for, but I was eager to discover why Rhonda had decided to lie about Lisa's diary.

An hour later, I was still wondering. Lisa Lane's diary was a testament to the shallow egocentrism of a girl who'd never relied on anything but her good looks. It was almost painful to read. It wasn't just the shallow nature of her musings but also how seriously she took herself that got to me. Maybe all of our journals are that way, I thought. Perhaps we're all pitifully self-absorbed.

Lisa's diary had two central themes: her looks and her love life. She was obsessed with her weight and dieted religiously. She lamented the smallness of her breasts, the largeness of her feet, the pointiness of her nose. She worried that her blond hair was starting to darken and spent hours lying in the sun with lemon in her hair and baby oil on her skin. She was almost as obsessed with other bodies as her own. She wished her breasts were more like Mary Jane's and her skin as dark as Rita Colby's. She wished she were as tall and slender as Sarah Ringer, and that she could be as strong and forceful as her, too.

When I read Sarah Ringer's name, my pulse quickened. So they *had* known each other. And Lisa had admired Sarah's physique and strength. It was the second time someone had described Sarah as a strong woman. Lauren had called her headstrong and gutsy. I wondered if Mary Jane was referring to Sarah's physical strength, or to her personality.

I read on. The other all-consuming theme in Lisa's life

was romance. She described the perfect mate in great detail, her large loopy letters filling page after page. She knew what she wanted in a man. She described the wedding ceremony, with three pages dedicated to her wedding dress alone. She knew how many children she wanted: two boys and a girl. She even had them named.

But as I read, I realized that Lisa's quest for the perfect mate had taken her along a disappointing path. She dated with a fervor that always ended in disaster. She fell head-over-heels in love time and again, only to be unceremoniously dumped or, more often, to find that the guy wasn't at all what she'd expected. She filled pages fretting about the best way to let her latest beau down without destroying his ego.

The list of names was dizzying, but from what I could tell, Lisa had been at least prudent enough not to be sleeping with all of them. In fact, the big breakup seemed to generally occur just before the loving couple consummated their union. Lisa wrote more than once that she believed in waiting for the right man, and that she'd know him when she found him. In the meantime, she didn't seem to mind doing everything short of actual copulation, and she described in great detail the kisses and fondling that took place with each of her dates.

It wasn't until the third to final entry that I found the first allusion to Markie Lewis. As with so many of her other love interests, Markie consumed her every waking moment. He was by far the "handsomest" guy she'd ever dated, she wrote. He had a "totally buff bod and sexy black hair that I'm dying to run my hands through!" Many of Lisa's sentences ended with exclamation points when referring to Markie. And it was in her final entry that I found what I thought was the reason Rhonda Lou had not wanted Lisa's diary to be found.

My whole body tingles, thinking about what's going to happen tonight! Of course, I may change my mind, but this time I think I'm really going to do it! Yesterday at rehearsal, Markie and I were kissing (he has the softest lips!) and I was putting my hands in his back pockets, and guess what I found? Cherry-flavored condoms!! You could tell he was all embarrassed, and so was I, but then later he asked me if I liked cherries — right in front of Rita and Mary Jane and I almost died!

I wish there was someone I could talk to about it, but there isn't. My pathetic roommate is about as square as they come. She's such a loser, no one would even want to have sex with her anyway, and every time I even go out on a date, she's all "Be careful!"

I can't talk to Bridget, even if she is my best friend, because she's all down about Brad and it would just make her envious that I've got someone when she doesn't. I can't really tell Mary Jane either, because she's already having sex with half the guys on campus, and she'll just think I'm a total virgin. And Rita Colby always acts so superior, I wouldn't feel comfortable talking to her. If Sarah were still alive, I'm pretty sure I could talk to her. Even though she could be uppity sometimes, I don't think she'd make me feel stupid the way Mary Jane would. But I can't bear to think about that. Even after all these months, I'm still so freaked out by what happened to poor Sarah I can hardly sleep sometimes. If it could happen to her, it could happen to anyone. She was so dynamic! I hope they catch whoever did that to her and make him fry in the electric chair! Or is it a gas chamber?

Anyway, I think I'll wear my new yellow sweater tonight. It's so cute! It's got little blue checks on it, and . . .

That was the final entry in Lisa Lane's diary. Obviously she'd been interrupted before being able to finish the all-important details of her evening attire.

I closed the diary and sat back against the love seat. Lisa Lane had been a shallow, even mean-spirited young woman about to embark on her first actual sexual encounter. Nothing in her diary intimated suicidal tendencies. Nor did there seem to be anything incriminating about anyone else. So who had wanted her diary and why? I thought I understood Rhonda's reluctance to let the diary be read. She'd considered Lisa her friend, and she'd been betrayed.

Suddenly I wondered about the last interrupted entry. Who'd interrupted her? Could Rhonda have found Lisa writing in her journal and then later not been able to stop herself from reading it? Could Lisa's betrayal of Rhonda been enough to set Rhonda off? I tried to picture Rhonda following Lisa to the party, confronting her on the beach, hitting her on the head and dragging her drugged body out into the surf, holding her head under until she drowned. Not a very likely scenario, I thought, picking up Rhonda's diary. What remained of my coffee was ice-cold and the M&M's were long gone.

Rhonda's writing surprised me. Lisa had called her pathetic, but I found her insights refreshing. She had a wry humor which she aimed as frequently at herself as at others. Like Lisa, she was obsessed with her weight. But she handled it differently.

Lisa asked me to go shopping with her today. Like right. I'm sure she'd enjoy hanging out at Pretty and Plump. Actually, she just hates going anywhere alone. I feel kind of bad for her. I mean, I know I was her last choice. She must be pretty desperate if she wants to go out with me. Usually she's embarrassed to be seen in public with me. I think she's afraid that people will think she's a loser if she's seen hanging with someone not suffering from anorexia. I told her I had to study and she tried to hide her relief. Asking me had obviously been a spontaneous action based on a moment of weakness. Now that I've said no, she's acting quite cheerful.

Whereas Lisa's diary had been a chronological accounting of events in her life, Rhonda's diary was more philosophical in nature. Lisa's quest had been to find the perfect mate. Rhonda's quest was directed toward self-awareness, with the same caustic eye she used in her photographs. My brief suspicion that Rhonda might have reacted violently to Lisa's cruel description of her was short-lived. Rhonda had known all along the type of person her roommate was. And she hadn't held it against her.

By the time I closed Rhonda's diary, I felt completely dirty. It was one thing to break into someone's house and go through their things when you suspect them of something criminal, but I'd just invaded the privacy of someone I instinctively liked. Someone who didn't deserve it. Rhonda had extended her friendship to me and I'd deceived and betrayed her.

I looked at my watch, surprised it was already late afternoon. It was too late to return the diaries to Rhonda's. I'd have to wait till morning. I started pacing the tiny room, restless and edgy. Something I'd read had triggered an idea and, as I paced, I tried to sort out the details I'd learned. Finally, I took out my notebook and started making a chart.

What did Lisa Lane have in common with Sarah Ringer? Moreover, what did Sarah have in common with the other serial victims? Even though I didn't really believe Lisa's death was related to the other three victims, I wrote all four names across the top of my chart, drawing vertical lines for columns. To the left, I began listing characteristics, and then marked Yes, No, or a question mark under each name.

All four women were young, but only Lisa and Sarah were college students. All four were slender but only Sarah and the last victim, Sally Thompson, were tall. Both Lisa and Sarah were blond, but the last two victims were brunettes. Sarah Ringer had been described as headstrong, gutsy and dynamic, none of which I thought applied to Lisa Lane. But what about Tracy Lee and Sally Thompson? Martha had never mentioned a thing about either woman's personality.

I stopped writing, and tapped my pencil against the

table. I checked my watch, grabbed a jacket and headed for the pay phone to call Martha.

When I couldn't reach her at home or work, I figured she'd headed back to Lincoln City. I could have paged her, but the last thing Martha needed was to be bothered. Instead, I jogged back to the apartment, hopped into my Jeep Cherokee and gunned it south onto Highway 101 toward Gold Beach. It was only four o'clock. If I hurried, I could make the trek in under two hours and reach the video store where Tracy Lee had worked by six o'clock.

Is that what the killer had done? I wondered. Did he wait till his work or school day was over, then hop in his truck or van and head off in one direction or another, searching for a victim? If so, how did he choose? I knew that serial killers often went after specific types, but these women didn't share many physical characteristics. So, maybe he went for certain personality types, I thought.

But then he couldn't just pick them randomly, could he? He'd have to get to know them. He'd have to stalk them, wouldn't he? Which meant he'd have to spend a lot of time in Gold Beach and Lincoln City. Wouldn't the women have noticed him hanging around? Unfortunately, both locations were tourist traps. Was that why he chose them? Because strange faces are more common in beach towns?

I let my mind continue in this vein as the miles sped past, and by the time I reached Gold beach, I had more questions than answers.

Like most of the beach towns on the Oregon Coast, this one stretched out along the highway and it didn't take me long to locate the mini-mall that housed Oscar's Videos where Tracy Lee had worked. I was relieved to see lights on inside and cars in the lot. In winter, when nights are long and cold, video rental stores do a booming business. I noticed that Oscar's stayed open until nine.

Inside, the movie shelves were draped with blue and

silver tinsel, lending the place a festive air. I watched as a tall, gangly clerk waited on a customer. Obviously the Christmas spirit hadn't wormed its way into his heart yet. He had a noticeably surly demeanor. I waited for the last two customers to leave before I approached him. Given his sour disposition, I decided that, for once, honesty would get me the quickest results.

"Hi," I said, flipping open my I.D. He peered at my detective's license like he'd seen a million of them. "Mind if I ask a few questions?"

"Again? Haven't you guys been here enough?" A shock of bleached blond bangs stuck out from beneath a Mariners cap, framing narrow green eyes. "This *is* about Tracy, right?"

"Right. How'd you guess?"

"Like anything else has happened here in a million years. You guys just keep coming back."

"Not me. I'm new. Those other guys were the cops. This won't take long at all. I just wondered if you could describe Tracy for me. You *did* know her?"

"Sure. Worked with her for nine months. She was an oriental chick. Dark hair . . ."

I cut him off. "Not physically. Personality-wise. What was she like?"

He tugged at his cap, then crossed his arms and leaned back against the opposite counter. "The truth? Tracy was kind of a bitch. Not all the time, but she could be. Bet you weren't expecting that for an answer, were you?" He seemed unduly pleased with himself.

"How do you mean? How was she a bitch?"

"Oh, you know. She was real full of herself. Kind of bossy. She didn't really put up with a lot of shit, if you know what I mean."

"Rude to customers?"

"Nah, not really. People mostly liked her. She was good-looking and all that. But if guys hit on her, she'd put them right in their place."

"You ever try to hit on her?"

He narrowed his eyes and stuck out his chin. "Fuck no." He stole a glance at the glass door as a mother and two little kids entered the store.

I lowered my voice. "Would you say Tracy was a strong woman?"

"If strong means pushy, sure."

"How about headstrong or uppity?"

"Yeah, she *was* those."

"Gutsy? Dynamic?"

"Yeah, yeah, all that. But she could be a bitch, too. I hate that everyone around here has turned her into some fucking saint. Trust me, you catch her at the wrong time of the month, she was bitchy as hell. I should know. I'm the one who had to work with her."

I thanked the asshole for his time and smiled all the way to my Jeep. Driving back to Kings Harbor all I could think about was that unless Martha told me Sally Thompson was some meek little mouse, we may have finally found the common link between the victims. And if the killer's type really was strong-willed, "pushy" women, Lisa Lane didn't match the killer's type one bit.

Chapter Fourteen

He was amazed that no one had noticed how often he was slipping into the dream phase while he went about his daily routine. It was happening more and more frequently, but what could he do? It was either this, or go find a new adventure. And as much as he longed to do just that, it was still too soon.

The good news was, he no longer had to close his eyes to remember. Even performing other tasks, he could sometimes envision the whole thing. But it was better if he broke it into segments, savoring each detail the way he had cherished that caramel sucker he'd once made last a whole month. Even as a little kid, he'd shown extraordinary patience and resolve.

He sighed, marveling at his own self-restraint, and let the final scene play itself out. He'd been saving this one. He swallowed before letting it roll.

He liked to play with them. Once he'd shown them who was boss, he could pretty much do as he pleased. This one hadn't taken long to quit resisting. She closed her eyes tight as he tickled the underflesh of her wrists all the way to her elbow. She tried not to cringe, because cringing turned him on. He knew she knew this, the same way he knew she knew that in the end he'd make her cringe to death. That's how he liked to think of it. He didn't kill them. He made them cringe to death.

He was aware of the time and knew he couldn't take forever. How he longed for a basement, some dark place where he could take her and keep her. Once he moved to a big city, that was the first thing he'd do. Then he'd never have to hurry again. But here on the Oregon coast, he had to be careful, had to keep moving. In small towns, people remembered things, people recognized you. So the van had become his death mobile. Some day soon, though, he'd be able to stretch out, and make things last.

He'd taken too long already. The morning light was already starting to ruin what had been a glorious night.

His van was parked on a lonely gravel road, beneath a stand of Douglas fir. Not one other vehicle had come this way all evening. But who knew what might happen in the light of day? He heaved a sigh. It was time to wrap this up.

"It's almost Thanksgiving," he said, surprised at the emotion in his voice.

She refused to look at him. Her swollen eyes, red from

the useless sobbing she'd long since abandoned, stared at the ceiling. But no amount of willpower could stop her body from shaking.

"Are you thankful?" he asked.

Dumbly, she nodded. Maybe she thought that this would be it. She clearly had no illusions of being spared. She probably only wished it would be over.

"I am so thankful I met you, Sally. You've made me so very happy. And you're not the least bit the way you used to be, are you?"

She dared to look up then and cringed at the sight of his lips still dripping with her blood. She couldn't remember where he'd bitten her last. Her whole body convulsed with pain and she could no longer differentiate between the bite marks. He knew this. Just as he knew it was time.

He leaned over her battered body and tenderly touched his slippery lips to hers. The lips were what he wanted. He sucked them into his mouth, bared his teeth and chomped down. Then, with loving fingers, he circled her thin neck and squeezed with all his might.

Chapter Fifteen

On Wednesday morning, it looked like the clouds had decided to settle in for the winter. If there was a sun up there, it wasn't going to show itself anytime soon. I'd finally reached Martha and we were sitting in a booth at the Tea Kettle Cafe, on the north end of Kings Harbor, warming our hands around coffee mugs.

"Okay, kiddo," she said. "I know that look. What have you found? And please tell me it's good news."

"First, tell me what Sally Thompson was like. Personality-wise."

She arched an eyebrow, then took out the small green notepad she carried in her jacket pocket, and flipped pages.

"Her mother said she was the perfect child," she said, "if that helps."

"Go on."

"Let's see. A co-worker, Diana Paige, described her as a real take-charge lady. Always on the go. A physical fitness buff. Her landlady had nothing but praise for her. Always paid the rent on time. The bus driver, who may have been the last one to see her alive, said she was haughty, if you can believe that. Since when do bus drivers use words like *haughty*? Anyway, I asked him what he meant and he said she had her nose in the air a lot. Thought she was too good to ride the bus."

"Yes!" I pounded my fist on the table, causing coffee to slosh out of our cups.

"You care to explain your sudden enthusiasm?" Martha said, wiping up the spill.

I told her about reading Lisa Lane's diary and her description of Sarah Ringer as a strong, dynamic, sometimes uppity woman. I told her that Dr. Monroe had described Sarah as headstrong and gutsy. Then I told her about my trip to Gold Beach and what the oh-so-pleasant video clerk had said about Tracy Lee being all of those things and more.

"You're saying our guy goes after uppity women?"

"Pushy broads, maybe. Women he sees as a threat."

"To his manhood?"

"Maybe. All three were dominant, independent types. Tracy Lee was known to *put men in their place*, according to the creep I talked to last night. Maybe she put our guy in his place. Maybe they all did."

The waitress set a platter piled high with pancakes in front of Martha, who continued to stare at me with amazement. "Shit," she muttered.

"There a problem, hon? You did say the high stack?" The waitress set my plate of eggs and bacon in front of me and looked anxiously at Martha.

"No, this is fine. I was thinking of something else."

The waitress sashayed away, and Martha sighed. "I can't believe I didn't see this," she grumbled.

"If we're right," I said, giving her equal credit for the idea since I could tell she was miffed at herself, "then I'll bet this guy stalks them. He finds someone who fits the mold, then follows them around, planning his attack. It's not like he sees a blonde and grabs her. He waits for someone to set him off, then stalks her."

Martha was nodding, starting to work on her pancakes. "I'll bet he trolls for them. Goes up and down the coast, waiting for someone to bite. Maybe days, or even weeks go by without anyone taking his bait. Then, when someone does, he starts reeling them in."

"But not Lisa Lane," I said. Martha looked up from her pancakes.

"Lisa was not dynamic," I explained. "She wasn't particularly strong-willed. She was petty, shallow and eager to please. She wasn't his type."

"And she wasn't mutilated, either. I know, I know. The M.O. doesn't match. But she did drown, and she did know the first victim. What if she knew something about the first victim that connected her to the killer? What if the killer knew this and decided Lisa was a liability? He wouldn't want to kill her like the others. That would attract too much attention."

"Okay, okay," I said, biting off a piece of bacon. "I'll keep digging up what I can on Lisa. Meanwhile, what's happening in Lincoln City?"

"A break, maybe. All the more reason you should stick with Lisa. You know how I told you this guy cleans up his victims? Pours ammonia on their vaginas and bite wounds? Leaves no prints, no pubic hairs? Well, this time, we found a minuscule hair sample on the condom. He'd washed it like the others, but beneath the knot where the condom was tied, we found a single hair fiber. You ready for the bombshell? On my own, I asked the M.E. who autopsied Lisa Lane to examine the hair found on Sally Thompson. I didn't expect a match, Cass. I'm just covering bases. Turns out there's a chance the hair does match the pubic hairs found on Lisa. At least, he can't rule it out. The color, thickness and texture match, but as the M.E. pointed out, a hell of a lot of people out there have black, curly pubic hair." She paused, gulping her coffee. "At least the terrible twins have sent the semen samples and hair in for DNA testing. I tried to get them to send a sample from Lisa, too, but they shined me on. These guys are really starting to tick me off."

Martha checked her watch, then blanched and reached for her wallet.

"My treat," I insisted. "Go. I'll wait for the check."

"Be careful, babe," she said, leaning over to peck my cheek. "And good work on the personality angle. I can't wait to see the Feds' reaction when they hear it."

I watched her march away with long purposeful strides and was stricken with a sudden, horrifying thought. Martha was exactly the type of woman the killer went for. And then, another thought hit me. So was I.

Chapter Sixteen

When I got back to campus, I spent an hour or so looking at vehicles in the parking lot closest to the P.A. building. If Martha was right about the perp's vehicle having wide tires, she had her work cut out for her. In the one parking lot alone, I counted twenty-seven vans, trucks and sports utility vehicles. Even some of the cars looked like they had sixteen-inch-wide tires. And this was the smallest lot on campus. I knew there were at least three others.

I gave up counting and headed for the theater, wondering at the nervousness I felt at the prospect of seeing Lauren again. Rehearsal was well underway and I watched from the back as the actors went through their dress rehearsal. I found myself glancing at Lauren, who was seated in her usual spot, taking notes in the dimly lit room. Damn, I thought. She even looked good in the dark.

The flats I'd painted were being used and worked well. I recognized some of the pants I'd hemmed and Mary Jane was wearing the silky shift that I'd had on in Lauren's living room. It seemed ages ago, I thought, remembering the way Lauren's fingers brushed my thighs while she pinned the hem. Blushing, I headed backstage to see if there was anything useful for me to do.

"Psst," Lauren hissed, getting my attention. I stopped, wondering if she could see my blush in the darkened room.

"I left you a note in the prop room," she said. She turned her attention back to the stage, and I hurried away.

As her note requested, I spent the next several hours color-coding cardboard boxes so the actors would be able to keep their costumes straight. No more tossing them randomly into a closet and searching for them later. Each actor was to have their own box, easily recognizable by its color. I think she was trying to punish me by finding the most tedious job she could think of.

I could tell that rehearsal was over by the sudden burst of laughter and voices backstage. Sealed away in my workroom, I tried to put faces to the voices and was surprised at how many I'd come to recognize. They seemed a happier group today, pleased with the way the rehearsal had gone, less contentious with one another. I waited for Lauren to come find me, and was strangely disappointed when she didn't. The voices were long gone by the time I'd painted the last box.

On the way back to the apartment, I stopped by the deli for another vegetarian special, half-afraid I'd run into Lauren, half-hoping I would. But the deli was nearly empty and I took the sandwich back to the apartment where I could work on my notes while I ate.

Markie had said he'd pick me up before five. What did

that mean? Four-thirty? Four-fifty-five? I got ready early and then paced the tiny apartment, anxious to get on with the evening. I couldn't wait to see the place where Lisa Lane had ended her life.

By the time Markie finally pulled up in a black Chevy truck, I was beginning to think I'd been stood up. I was halfway out the door when he tooted his horn unnecessarily. Classy guy, Markie. I pulled myself up into the passenger's seat and managed a weak smile.

"Didn't see you at rehearsal today," he said, giving me the once-over. "I was afraid maybe you'd skipped town." He chuckled at this and reached over to squeeze my knee. It took great restraint not to smack him.

"I went in early to do some painting. When I left, rehearsal was well underway. How'd it go, anyway?"

"Pretty good, actually. Professor Pervert had a major cow, though. He and Brad got into a shouting match. You should've been there. I thought the professor was going to bust an artery, the way he was screaming. It was funny as hell."

"What was he so mad about?" I wished Markie would start watching the road. I hate drivers who feel they need to make eye contact while talking with the passengers. I was about to rip the steering wheel out of his hands.

"Oh, it was all a misunderstanding, actually. The professor thought Brad was acting inappropriately with Mary Jane, but he wasn't. Mary Jane and him go way back, but how was the professor supposed to know that? Anyway, Mary Jane kind of slapped Brad, which was funny all by itself, and then Professor Pervert leaps up onto the stage and charges at Brad like he's fucking Zorro or something. 'Unhand her!' he screams. It was hilarious."

"He really said that?"

Markie nodded and swerved, narrowly missing a red Volkswagen in the oncoming lane. We were only going about thirty miles an hour, but the road was winding and a head-on collision didn't appeal to me.

109

"He goes, 'You will not be permitted to conduct yourself in this manner in this theater!' or some such horseshit, and Brad, who was kind of embarrassed because Mary Jane had slapped him in the first place, says 'Hey, chill, Purvis. This is something personal between me and the lady. It's got nothing to do with this theater, okay?' "

Markie's true talent was obviously impersonation. I could easily picture the whole scene. The problem was, he used both hands while he spoke which meant they were nowhere near the steering wheel a good part of the time. I suspected my face was ashen.

"What did Purvis do?" I asked, pointedly looking at the road, hoping he'd get the hint.

"Purvis looked like he was going to explode. His face went all red and his eyes sort of popped out like this." Markie screwed his face up and looked at me with bulging eyes.

Despite myself, I laughed.

"Then he goes, 'That's *Mister* Purvis to you, son. Now either you conduct yourself appropriately or you are not welcome here. And apologies are in order. To Miss Mary Jane, to myself and to the entire cast and orchestra. We've all put up with your nonsense far too long. Either apologize right now or get out!' "

"What did Brad do?"

"He goes, 'Hey, I'm sorry. Okay?' and like everyone else knew he wasn't sincere, but Purvis, he just bobbed his head that way he does and turned away, all smug like he'd done something real important. The guy's a total joke."

To my relief, Markie finally brought the truck to a stop and turned off the engine. He looked at me with dancing eyes, clearly enthralled with his own performance. "You shoulda been there." He reached over and tapped the same knee he'd squeezed earlier. I wondered how long I'd be able to put up with his nonsense before I hauled off and decked him.

"So this is it?" I asked, looking around at the towering sand dunes. There were no other vehicles in sight and I was beginning to think I'd made a bad decision in coming.

"Just over this hill. Most people park on the north side and walk up, but I like to drive in as far as I can. You'll see. Come on, help me carry this stuff up."

I climbed out of the truck and sank to my ankles in fine white sand. For once, I was glad I was wearing my new clodhoppers. Markie handed me two beach chairs and a small portable radio. Then he hefted a large ice chest onto his shoulder and led the way.

It didn't take me long to conclude that climbing sand dunes is right up there with going to the dentist, in terms of sheer pleasure. By the time we reached the knoll, I was winded, grouchy, and the backs of my calves ached. But when we reached the top, I was rewarded with a breathtaking sight.

The dunes rose in white billowy mounds nearly two hundred feet before arcing gracefully toward the pounding surf below. On the west-facing slopes, the ocean winds had carved intricate designs into the fine sand, giving them texture and depth. Surprisingly, tall stands of fir and spruce sprang up like island forests, and here and there the sand was covered with beach grass, bent eastward from the powerful coastal winds. But at the moment, the air was still and only the sound of the pounding surf filled the air.

"Wait till it gets darker," Markie said, clearly enjoying my reaction to the view. "The whole sky lights up with stars, and the moon shines on the waves like gold glitter. It's awesome. Of course, tonight the clouds might be too thick to see any of that."

Which was the understatement of the year, I thought, looking up at the darkening mass overhead. All day long the clouds had continued to gather, and now it looked as though it might rain at any minute.

"Don't worry about rain," Markie said, reading my mind. "Come on, you'll see what I mean."

"We're not there yet?" I dreaded another trek through the sand. Markie just grinned and there was nothing to do but to follow him.

Just over a small hummock, I was relieved to find a surprisingly large gathering of people. Several were erecting a huge tent-like awning while others worked at getting a bonfire started with driftwood. Sand chairs were spread out around the firepit, and ice chests served as tables for cans and bottles.

"Wow," I said.

"Cool, huh? Go ahead and set up our chairs. I'll get us a beer."

I looked around for someone I knew and spotted Rita Colby standing off by herself, staring at the ocean. I decided to join her.

"It's beautiful," I said, standing beside her. She looked up, clearly surprised to see me.

"It used to be. Now I'm not so sure."

"Why's that?"

"This is where a friend of mine died a few weeks ago. I haven't been back since then. It just all seems so different."

"I heard about that. Were you and Lisa good friends?"

Rita's dark eyes appraised me, and then she turned back toward the ocean. "Not really," she said, letting out a short laugh. "It seems like now that she's dead, everyone who ever met her considers her one of their closest friends. But really, I never liked her that much. She was, oh, I don't know how to say this, somewhat one-dimensional. You know what I mean?"

I told her I did.

"Still, though, it freaks me out that she died that way. I can't imagine what possessed her to go swimming that night. If it had been summer, maybe. But November? I just don't get it."

"Maybe someone went with her?" I suggested. "And they're not telling because they don't want anyone to think they're responsible for her death."

Rita looked at me again, those dark eyes shining in the dusk. Her black curly hair was pulled back in a ponytail in a vain attempt to control the unruly mass, but several tendrils had broken loose and seemed alive with electricity. Slowly, she nodded. "I admit, that thought has crossed my mind a lot. And it's not like I don't have my suspicions. She was with Mark Lewis that night. I saw them heading back toward the trees and it was pretty obvious what was on their agenda. She was pretty high, it looked like. Giggling like crazy. But then, not that much later, I saw Markie, so I just don't know. I mean, I remember wondering where Lisa had gone. Actually, I thought at first that maybe she'd changed her mind and that's why Markie was back drinking beer with his buddies. I thought maybe she'd gone home. But I'm sure the police went over all the possibilities. If they didn't find anything wrong, I guess I should just leave it alone."

"You don't sound convinced, though."

"It's just that, well, it's not like Markie to give up that easily. He doesn't like taking no for an answer. I should know." She hugged her jacket around her and shuddered.

"You and Mark Lewis were lovers?" I asked.

Her laughter came out like a bark. "Hardly. You ever hear of date rape?"

"You're kidding," I said. From her expression, I realized I'd used a poor choice of words. "Did you tell anyone? Go to the police?"

"Hell, I was the one who started it. I thought he was a hunk. I might have even enjoyed it, had he given me the chance. The asshole got me so drunk I didn't know what I

113

was doing. The next thing I knew, he was on top of me and I couldn't get him off. It was over in a matter of minutes."

"Jesus," I said. "You think that's what happened to Lisa?"

"Lisa wasn't acting like someone who was being forced," she said. "She was practically hanging on him. Had been for a couple of weeks. The way I figure it, they went into the trees, did the nasty, he comes back for a couple of beers and she decides to take a dip in the ocean. The only problem is, how come he never went looking for her? How come he stayed around drinking beer with Brad till two in the morning? That's the part I don't get."

"Am I interrupting something?" The voice made us both jump and I wheeled around. Markie was holding out an open Budweiser to me.

"I see you two have met," he said, letting his gaze rove Rita's body. She glared back at him, her eyes like hot coals.

"Obviously, so have you two," Rita said.

"Markie offered to give me a ride tonight," I said hurriedly.

"Well, don't let me keep you. I've just discovered I'm not really in the party mood."

I watched in dismay as Rita Colby disappeared across the sloping sand and down an embankment.

"Oh, don't mind her," Markie said. "She's just jealous. She used to have this thing for me, but she's really not my type."

Only my resolution to see my part through stopped me from slugging him right then and there and following Rita away from the party.

Instead, I followed Markie back toward the firepit, searching the crowd for the red-headed Bridget. From Lisa's diary, I had a fairly good description of the girl she claimed was her closest friend. Red wavy hair, blue eyes, light-complected skin with a smattering of freckles across her nose. I found her off away from the fire, talking to the buxom Mary Jane.

"I'll be back in a minute," I said to Markie.

"Well, don't disappear on me," he said, patting my backside. I gritted my teeth and willed myself not to react. There'd be time enough to set Markie Lewis straight before this was all over. Right now, I needed to play him along.

"Hi," I said, walking up to Mary Jane and Bridget. "Mind if I join you? I don't know hardly anyone here."

"Looks to me like you got to know Markie Lewis pretty fast," Bridget said. Her light blue eyes flashed with anger.

"Hey, he just offered me a ride," I said. "It's not like we're dating or anything." She continued to glare at me, and I took a sip of my beer. This was going to be more difficult than I'd thought.

"It's not your fault," Mary Jane said. Up close, she wasn't quite as pretty as onstage. Her long, curly brown hair framed a round face accented by pointy ears and a sharply upturned nose. Her pouty lips were coated in red lip gloss, making her mouth the focal point of her face. It was the knockout body that gave the illusion of beauty.

"Markie was dating Bridget's best friend, that's all. The one who drowned two weeks ago. It's pretty hard to see him show up with another girl, like nothing ever happened."

"God, I'm sorry," I said. "I had no idea. Markie was dating Lisa?"

Bridget nodded and sniffled. She looked like she was ready to cry. "She made love to him that night. She didn't tell me, but I know she did. I could tell she was going to. She wouldn't even look at me. That's how I knew for sure what she was planning. She didn't think I'd approve." Bridget started to cry and Mary Jane put her arm around her, patting the redhead's shoulder.

"You were her best friend. She'd have told you

115

eventually. Probably the next day. Anyway, Markie denies they had sex. For Markie Lewis, that's a minor miracle. Usually he brags about it whether it's true or not."

"He's probably just trying to protect himself," Bridget said. "Afraid someone will think she killed herself over him. But I know she wouldn't do that. She would never take her own life."

"When's the last time you saw her?" I asked. They both looked at me quizzically. "I mean, it seems strange no one saw her," I added hastily.

"When I saw them go into the woods, I just left," Bridget said. "I wasn't going to sit around and watch my best friend make a fool of herself. Markie Lewis only wanted one thing from Lisa, and as soon as he got it, he'd dump her for someone new. Lisa was smart about some things, but when it came to men, she was an idiot." Bridget's pale freckled face was blotched with emotion.

"How about you?" I asked Mary Jane. Her face also reddened and she looked down at the ground. Then she took a long swallow of her beer. "Sorry, I didn't mean to get personal," I said.

"No, it's okay. Gosh, everyone else seems to know anyway. I was with Brad that night. We used to go together a long time ago. Anyway, I thought he'd changed, but he hasn't. He's still the same self-centered jerk he always was. He can be so sweet sometimes, when he wants to."

"When he wants something from you is more like it," Bridget spat.

"Yeah, I guess that's true. But I'm not as smart as you. At least you knew how to say no."

A look passed between the two women and then Bridget started to giggle.

"What?" Mary Jane asked.

Bridget was laughing too hard to answer. She plunked down onto the sand, holding her sides, and Mary Jane and I sat down beside her.

116

"What?" Mary Jane demanded again. Suddenly, her eyes widened. "You and Brad? You did, didn't you? Oh, my god. You and Brad did it!"

Bridget nodded, trying to get her giggles under control.

"What's so funny?" I asked.

"Bridget has been lecturing me for months about the dangers of casual sex," Mary Jane said. "And all along, she was holding back." She crossed her arms across her impressive chest.

I looked a question at her.

"Bridget and Brad dated after he and I broke up," she explained. "Now she's saying they did more than date." With flashing eyes, she turned to face Bridget. "I don't believe you."

"It's true," Bridget insisted, still laughing. "Just once, though. Once was enough." She was struggling to catch her breath.

"Prove it," Mary Jane said. She thrust out her lower lip in a pout.

"How? You don't believe me? Why would I lie about something like that? It's not like I'm proud of it." Bridget's pale complexion darkened.

"When?" Mary Jane asked. "Where?"

"God, Mary Jane. You act like you're jealous. It was just after you two broke up the first time. It's not like I knew you'd ever date him again. Anyway, it happened over there, about two dunes from here." She pointed in the direction where Markie had parked the truck.

"Why didn't you tell me?" Mary Jane asked.

"I was ashamed," Bridget said, looking at the ground. All three of us drank our beers.

Suddenly, Mary Jane perked up. "Afterwards, did he do anything odd?" Her dark eyes were wide and mischievous. I wondered at this change.

Bridget's eyes narrowed and then she threw back her head and started laughing again, her red hair shimmering as her shoulders shook.

117

"What?" I asked. Mary Jane had started to laugh too. The two of them seemed to be enjoying a private joke.

"Does he always do that?" Bridget asked. "I mean, did he do that with you?"

Mary Jane nodded, her eyes brimming. "Every single time," she said. "God, I've been dying to tell someone."

"What?" I asked. These two were driving me crazy.

"You tell," Mary Jane said. I wondered if she were somehow still testing Bridget, still not really believing that her friend had slept with Brad.

"After he's through," Bridget said, lowering her voice and looking back toward the fire, "he pulls off the condom and ties a little knot in the end, keeping all his, you know, stuff, inside it. Then he says something and heaves it as far as he can across the dunes."

"What does he say?" I asked, my head suddenly spinning. The two women looked at each other and broke into spontaneous laughter.

"Bombs away!" they said in unison, and they both lobbed imaginary sperm-filled condoms over the hill.

It wasn't just this news that had my head reeling. I noticed I was starting to have difficulty formulating clear, cohesive thoughts. I looked at the beer I was drinking. It was nearly empty. But one beer never had this kind of effect on me. I looked at Mary Jane and noticed that her face was fuzzy. So was Bridget's, for that matter. In fact, everything around me had suddenly taken on a soft, distorted halo. Suddenly, I felt ill.

"Hey, are you okay?" Bridget asked. Her red hair looked orange, like the distant fire.

"Gonna be sick," I said, struggling to my feet and heading for the stand of trees behind us. It was partly true, but more than the nausea propelling me forward was the sudden realization that I needed to get rid of whatever was in my system.

"She probably drank too much," I heard one of them

say. I could no longer distinguish between their voices. Nor could I stop to tell them they were wrong. I hadn't drunk too much. Someone had doctored my beer. Despite my addled condition, I remembered what Martha had told me about Rohypnol and I'd have bet anything that someone had slipped me a roofie.

I was still kneeling in the sand, trying to clear my senses, when I heard someone tromping through the dunes toward me. My stomach actually felt better, and my head had quit spinning, but I was nowhere near back to normal. I ducked behind a fir tree and peered through the darkness. To my dismay, it was Markie Lewis.

"Cassidy?" he called softly. I noticed he had two more beers in his left hand. "Ready or not, here I come," he said, his voice a teasing singsong. It sent shivers up my spine.

I started moving backwards, keeping my eye on his approaching form, keeping behind the trees as much as possible. My coordination wasn't good, but my instincts were. I did not want to be alone in the wooded dunes with Markie Lewis. Not with my senses dulled and my mind muddied with drugs.

Was this how it happened with Lisa Lane? I wondered. Had Markie slipped her a roofie, then taken her off into the woods? Had he left her there to sleep it off? Or had she fought back? Maybe she'd hit her head in the struggle. Maybe Markie had had to carry her all the way to the ocean, just to make it look like she'd drowned. Except the autopsy report said she *had* drowned. My mind was a jumble of conflicting thoughts as I backed my way out of the woods and over the crest of a dune. Once out of Markie's line of sight, I turned and ran as fast as I could.

Which wasn't saying much. The soft sand sucked at my feet, pulling me down to my knees time and again. My ankle-high boots were half-filled, weighing me down. But worst of all, I had no idea where I was going, no idea where I was. Waves of dizziness kept washing over me, and my vision was still blurred. And then, to make matters worse, it started to rain.

The first drops were fat and slow, plunking out of the sky like soggy hail. But in no time, the skies opened up and it began to pour in earnest. With the icy rain came a westerly wind that drove in sheets against my back and neck. My hair was plastered to my head, and as I ran, I held my arms around me to keep out the cold. Not only was I freezing, I was angry and confused. But underneath it all, mostly I was afraid.

Dune after dune, I trudged through the sand, my legs aching with the effort. I was fairly certain I was headed in the right direction, toward the road. Now and then, when I crested the top of a dune and looked back, I could see the glow of the bonfire, hear the voices beneath the tent. And I also thought I could see a lone figure, coming after me, following my footsteps in the sand as easily as if I'd left a lighted path.

Just when I thought I couldn't go another step, a strip of asphalt sprouted up out of nowhere. Relief washed over me and I pushed myself forward. I was almost to the road when the sound of an engine caught me by surprise. I hadn't seen any lights. Instinctively, I dove to the ground, tasting the salty sand, as I watched a dark van slip down the road, its lights off, its engine purring in the night like a dark secret.

For a brief moment, I thought of hailing a ride. But something stopped me. As foggy as my mind was, I knew there was something odd about the van's presence. Even drugged and soaked to the bone, I knew not to ignore the hairs on the back of my neck. They were practically standing at attention.

Once the van disappeared, I emptied the sand from my boots, struggling to pull them back on and retie the laces. Then, my breathing less ragged, I began jogging in the same direction. The feel of firm ground was a blessed relief after wading through the dunes. I kept my head down and splashed my way through the storm, ignoring the pounding of my overworked lungs and heart. When I saw the beam of headlights brighten the road in front of me, I dove into the ditch along the road.

The truck was heading the same direction as I was, about a half block behind me. Thank God the headlights had splashed the road, giving me fair warning. An instant later and he'd have probably spotted me.

I lay crouched in the ditch, letting the icy water pound my back while I waited for the truck to crawl by. Markie had a flashlight and was shining it in both directions along the road. I held my breath, willing my heart to slow down. If he saw me, I wasn't sure how much of a fight I'd be able to put up. I'd pretty much exhausted my last ounce of energy.

But the black truck inched past me and continued down the road. I watched his flashlight beams scanning the ground, searching for me. When at last Markie's truck was out of my view, I dragged myself out of the ditch. I alternated between jogging and walking, catching my breath when I could, listening through the pounding rain for the sound of an engine, knowing he could double back with his lights off and trick me, if I wasn't careful.

By the time I reached the main road, I was shivering uncontrollably. I was right on the edge of campus, and without thinking, without hesitating one bit, I headed for the closest safe place I knew.

Chapter Seventeen

"Cassidy!" Lauren's face told me all I needed to know about my appearance.

"Can I come in?" My lips were trembling and my knees had started to wobble. She threw the door open wide and pulled me into the entryway. A puddle immediately formed beneath my sodden clothes.

"My God, you're freezing. Let's get you out of those clothes."

I bent over to untie my boots and nearly collapsed. Lauren bent over to help me.

"My my, what have we here?" A voice came from

behind us. I looked up and saw a tall, silver-haired amazon peering down at me. At first I thought she was a man. "Don't tell me," she said. "This must be the new teacher's assistant you told me about. Yes?"

"Gracie, this is Cassidy James. Help me get her other boot. She needs to get in the shower."

"Oh, you seem to be doing just fine. I'll put some water on for tea." Gracie disappeared around the corner and, through chattering teeth, I apologized.

"I shouldn't have just dropped in," I said. "But I didn't know where else to go."

"Shhh. Don't talk. Let's get you under hot water, and then when you're warm and dry, you can tell us all about it." She led me, still dripping, into the bathroom and pushed me inside. "I'll get you a clean towel. Are you okay? I mean, you *can* stand under the water by yourself? You look a little wobbly."

I smiled reassuringly but sagged against the wall when she closed the door behind her. Slowly, I peeled off my clothes and heaped them in the sink so they wouldn't drip onto the hardwood floor. The fluffy bath mat felt so warm and soft beneath my feet I was tempted just to sit down on it. But I reached into the shower and turned on the hot water.

I was about to step into the shower when the door opened again. Lauren had a folded pink bath towel and a huge white terry robe in her arms. She seemed surprised to find me standing naked in front of her. Like a deer frozen in headlights, she stood gaping at my nakedness.

"I, uh, thought you were in the shower," she stammered. "I brought you these."

"Thanks," I said. Despite my weakened condition, Lauren's frank appraisal sent tingles of pleasure straight through me. It seemed an eternity while we stood gazing at each other. I couldn't move and Lauren seemed unable to tear herself away. When her eyes met mine again, I felt

123

something tug at my insides making them somersault in a downward spiral. Finally, she backed out the door, closing it softly without uttering a word.

I have rarely been so grateful for hot water as I was that night. I stood beneath the pounding jets, letting the water sluice down my aching body as it stung my icy skin. I washed my hair with some of Lauren's shampoo, which felt sinfully intimate. I ran soap over my body, luxuriating in the soft fragrance. I let the water stream into my mouth and drank as if I were dying of thirst. At last, I turned off the water and stepped out of the shower.

Now that I was no longer in danger and no longer freezing, I was able to more accurately assess the effect of the Rohypnol in my system, if that's what it was. There was no doubt in my mind that I had been drugged. My legs were still weak, and I felt both giddy and lethargic. My pupils were dilated, and although my vision had cleared, I could tell my coordination was off. It seemed to take me forever just to dry myself off, and I kept teetering. Also, I had trouble getting my mind to stay focused on any one thing. My thoughts bounced around like Ping-Pong balls, and I found myself giggling for no reason.

"You okay in there?" Lauren asked, obviously not daring to open the door.

I giggled and opened it myself. I could tell she was afraid to look, but I was safely wrapped in the white terry robe, as pink and scrubbed as a newborn.

"Better?" she asked.

"Much," I said. "I'm not sure what to do with my clothes." To my dismay, I realized my words were a tad slurred. Lauren cocked an eyebrow but ushered me into the living room.

"I'll throw them in the dryer," she said. "Gracie fixed you some tea."

Gracie looked like someone who'd sooner chop wood

than fix tea, but sure enough she handed me a steaming mug and motioned me toward the sofa.

"So, Lauren tells me you're quite the seamstress," she said, grinning. She had gray eyes that matched her hair, and the dark, tawny skin of an American Indian. The muscles in her shoulders and arms bunched beneath the black T-shirt she wore, and I had to admire her physique. Even clothed, she obviously didn't have an ounce of fat on her body.

"I'm afraid you'll be able to identify all the clothes I hemmed by the blood dots along the bottom," I said, sipping the tea. Was it my imagination, or had Gracie laced my tea with the tiniest bit of bourbon? Probably not the best combination with Rohypnol, but it tasted marvelous.

"And I also understand you saved our Miss Lauren from sure disaster. Ladder-climbing is not her forté."

"So I noticed." I couldn't get a fix on Gracie. Her gray eyes regarded me with humor but also suspicion. And what was the world's greatest homophobe doing with this amazon? First a gay brother and now Gracie-the-Wonder-Butch!

There was no denying the way Lauren had looked at me in the bathroom. Was there? I couldn't trust myself to be sure. The Ping-Pong balls were all over the place.

"What happened?" Lauren asked, coming into the living room. Gracie had fixed them tea as well, and Lauren took hers to the chair between us. I noticed that she did not choose to sit next to Gracie on the little love seat. Did this mean they weren't lovers?

"Did you ever hear of date rape?" I asked. Both women's eyes widened, and Gracie's hands curled into fists. Before I misled them further, I went on. "Someone laced my beer tonight with something I think was Rohypnol. Since Markie Lewis is the one who gave me the beer, I'm betting on him. When I went off into the trees to get sick,

125

he followed me. I started running, and he chased me. He even got in his truck and came after me. He knows where I live, which is why I didn't want to go back home tonight."

They were both looking at me strangely. "Are you sure he wasn't just coming after you to make sure you were okay?" Lauren asked.

I realized there was no way I could tell them about Lisa Lane having Rohypnol in her system, since that wasn't public knowledge. Unless I told them who I really was.

"I've heard of that drug," Gracie said, sipping her tea. "It's not just a cheap high," she said to Lauren. "It's the biggest date rape drug there is. No taste, no odor. A guy slips it into a girl's drink, and the next thing she knows, she wakes up in his bedroom. Sort of the Spanish Fly of the Nineties. If that's really what he gave you," she said, looking at me, "you're damn lucky you're here."

"Do you want to call the police?" Lauren asked. I could tell she still wasn't sure that I was right about Markie.

"And report what? Even you think Markie was just following after me to see if I needed help. I couldn't prove anything. No, I'd rather wait and deal with Markie my own way, in my own time."

"You need any help, you just holler," Gracie said, flexing her fingers. "This guy sounds like someone I need to meet." There was no mistaking the menace in her voice.

"Are you sure you're okay?" Lauren asked. She seemed genuinely concerned.

"Nothing a good night's sleep won't cure. I was hoping I could borrow your couch for the night. But if it's too much trouble, I've got a friend in town I can call."

"Don't be ridiculous," Gracie volunteered before Lauren could respond. "There's no way I'd let you leave here tonight. Lauren's got plenty of room, don't you, hon?"

Hon? My heart sank a little at the endearment.

"Uh, sure. I can make up the bed in the spare

bedroom for you. It won't take a minute." Her words were kind, but her face seemed unsure.

"The couch is fine. That way I can be out of your hair first thing tomorrow morning, before you're even up. I really appreciate this. I never intended to barge in on you this way."

"Please, enough apologizing," Gracie said, standing. "I was on my way out anyway. And the circumstances aside, I'm glad I got to meet you. Our professor here has done nothing all evening but talk of your heroics."

Lauren turned an appealing shade of crimson which she tried to cover by rolling her eyes at Gracie. "Gracie exaggerates all the time. It's a character flaw." She got up and walked Gracie to the door. I couldn't quite make out their words, but Gracie's low chuckle sounded warm and teasing. When Lauren came back into the room, she avoided my eyes.

"I'm sorry I chased your friend off like that," I said. Lauren took the empty mugs into the kitchen and I got up to follow. "She seems nice, though," I added when she ignored me.

"Gracie's as sweet as they come," she said, sighing. "As long as you don't get her angry. People who get on her bad side aren't likely to forget it soon. She's the only person I know who's proud of holding grudges."

"You two been together long?" I asked.

"What?" Lauren whirled around, surprised. Then she laughed. "Gracie is a dear friend of my brother's. That's how we met. I've only known her for about six months. Has anyone ever told you that you make a lot of assumptions?"

Actually, they had. I followed her into the living room and watched as she pulled the sofa down into a pull-out bed. I should have left things alone until I could think more rationally, but the Rohypnol had clouded my judgment and I was still angry about the other day.

"Maybe I do make too many assumptions," I said,

getting warmed up. "I should never have assumed, for example, that just because you have a gay brother, you'd be sensitive and open to other gays."

"Cassidy, you misinterpreted my reaction," she started, not turning around.

I cut her off. "I suppose I misinterpreted the way you looked at me in there, too," I said. "In the bathroom." I could hardly believe my words. Just that fast, my face had gone instantly hot. Lauren stood stock still, her back to me, neither of us breathing.

"I don't know what you mean," she said finally.

"Yes, you do. You know exactly what I mean. It was in your eyes, Lauren. You looked at me with, I don't know, longing. Disgust one day, longing the next. I don't get it."

"I'm afraid you're mistaken on both counts." Her words were clipped and feeble. She began slinging sheets onto the bed. My head was pounding in rhythm with my heart. *Could* I have been mistaken? Perhaps I'd just wanted her to look at me that way. Had I seen something that wasn't there?

Suddenly overwhelmed with embarrassment, I wheeled around toward the kitchen. To my utter dismay, the terrycloth belt of my robe caught on the sofa bed's hinge and pulled the robe completely open.

"Damn!" I bent over, fumbling to pull the belt free. Lauren's gaze met mine and her face went instantly pink once more.

"Jesus," she said, staring.

I struggled with the belt, feeling my own face flush. Every fiber of my being was humming, and I was intensely aware of her scrutiny. Finally, she pulled her gaze back up to meet my eyes.

"And that look right there," I said, my voice cracking. "Did I imagine that one too?"

Her face turned scarlet. "I have no idea what you're talking about. If you need extra blankets, they're in the linen closet." With that, she turned on her heel, switching off lights as she disappeared down the hallway.

"The only thing worse than a homophobic straight woman is a homophobic lesbian," I muttered. I knew she hadn't heard me, though. What would have been the point? I threw myself on the sofa bed and pulled the blankets up over my head, willing the dreadful night to come to an end.

Chapter Eighteen

Rain still droned against the windows and the sky was a leaden mess, but even so the clouds had lightened enough for me to realize that morning had blessedly arrived. I folded the sheets and blankets and slipped into the clothes Lauren had dried and left folded beside the couch.

Determined not to wake her, I decided against putting on my boots until I was outside. I slid open the deadbolt, turned the knob and stepped out onto the porch, holding my breath. As soon as I did, I nearly screamed. There was a man sitting six inches from the door.

"I hope this is as promising as it looks," he said,

giving me a lopsided smile. I glanced down at the boots in my hand and ran fingers through my uncombed hair.

"Afraid not," I said.

Even with the weight loss, there was no question that this was Lauren's brother, Corey. He looked enough like her to make my heart skip, and I realized with a pang that the heart is not to be trusted. After what had happened last night, how could my damned heart be so naive? It made me furious.

"I'm Corey," he said. "Want to join me for breakfast?" He held out a Dunkin' Donuts bag and offered me a peek inside. I sat down on the porch beside him and rummaged through the bag, pulling out a chocolate cruller. Until that second, I hadn't realized how famished I was.

"I'm Cassidy," I said, biting into the doughnut. "Has anyone ever told you that your timing's impeccable? Another minute and I would've starved to death."

"My sister didn't feed you?" His blue eyes twinkled mischievously, and I got an inkling of what Lauren would look like if she weren't so damned uptight.

"I'm afraid I was an uninvited guest. I sort of crashed a private party."

He raised an eyebrow and sipped from a large Styrofoam cup. The rain continued to pound the pavement, but under the porch roof we were quite protected.

"Here, I brought this for Lauren, but seeing as she's obviously still sleeping, you may as well have it." He handed me a second steaming cup and I gratefully swallowed coffee. Then I told him about last night's events.

"This is the guy who plays Judas in the musical?" he asked, chomping on a cinnamon roll. I nodded. "I knew that guy was a creep. When Lauren told me what happened to that girl, Lisa Lane, the first thing I told her was, 'I bet old Judas had something to do with it.' You should've gone to the police."

"Can you keep a secret?" I asked, feeling my heart accelerate even as I spoke. I knew I was about to do something I might regret, but right then Corey Monroe seemed like the only friend I had, and my gut instinct told me he was as trustworthy as they came. I looked into his intelligent blue eyes and saw what I needed. So I told him who I really was and what I was doing and why. He listened thoughtfully, nodding now and then as if the whole thing made perfect sense to him.

"So do you think the serial killings really could be related to Lisa's death?" he asked when I'd finished.

"I don't know what to think," I admitted. "I think Markie Lewis might have accidentally killed Lisa Lane. But I found out something else last night that puts a whole new light on things. I can't tell you, though, so please don't ask, okay?" Corey nodded, still looking solemn and trustworthy. "Can I ask you something weird?"

"We haven't got to the weird part?" He smiled.

"Trust me, it's about to get weirder." I sipped coffee, then plunged ahead. "Is it usual, I mean, have you ever heard of guys, uh, saving their semen in a condom after sex? You know, like tying one end of the thing like a balloon? Is that something guys do?"

"None of the guys I know," he said, furrowing his brow.

It was just too strange, I thought. I couldn't wait to tell Martha about Brad Caper's little ritual after sex. But could the guy who played Jesus be the serial killer? From what I'd seen of him, he could be both cruel and egotistical. But was he capable of those hideous crimes? Moreover, could he have killed Lisa Lane? Mary Jane had said she'd been with Brad the night that Lisa drowned. But later people had seen Brad and Markie together until almost two in the morning. Could the two of them be in it together?

While I sat there musing, Corey had started to chuckle. "What?" I asked.

"It's too funny, that's all. Here my sister is fretting

over these feelings she has for you, and all because you're a student, and all the time you're not really a student at all. I wish I could tell her."

"What are you saying, Corey?" I couldn't help it. My heart had done a miniature pirouette when he said this.

"For two days, she's been talking nonstop about this teaching assistant named Cassidy James. Cassidy this, Cassidy that. One thing about Lauren, she's a terrible liar. When I asked her if this was what I thought it was, she practically keeled over denying it. Which was, of course, how I knew that it was. But considering what happened at Stanford, I can't blame her for being gun-shy."

"What happened at Stanford?" I asked.

"Don't hate me for this, okay? But I can't tell. I mean, it's not my story to tell, it's hers. Let me just say that Lauren's last love interest ended in disaster, and the idea of getting involved with a student is way, way down on her list of priorities. You can imagine my surprise when I saw you sneak out of her house just now. I thought the ice queen had finally melted."

"Nope," I said. "Safely frozen, no thaw in sight. In fact, we sort of got into a disagreement last night. I've been getting some pretty mixed messages."

Corey laughed. "I can imagine."

"What about Gracie?" I asked.

"You met Gracie?" He was clearly delighted. "Isn't she the greatest? Don't worry, though. Gracie and Lauren have no romantic ties whatsoever. Believe me, I'd know. Besides, Gracie's happily married to Doreen."

Just then the door opened and we both turned to see Lauren gaping at us from the doorway. She was clad in a pink fluffy robe and slippers, and her hair was a tousled mess. I thought she looked sexy as hell.

"Good morning," Corey said cheerfully. "We saved you one doughnut."

Lauren continued to look from her brother to me,

133

apparently unable to process the image. "Aren't you two freezing out here?" she said at last, managing to regain her composure.

"Actually, yes," Corey said. "But Cassidy and I have had a wonderful time exchanging secrets, haven't we?"

"Best time I've had in ages," I agreed. "Thanks again for letting me barge in on you last night." I got to my feet. "And thank *you*," I said to Corey. I reached out to shake his hand, but he grabbed me in a bear hug and held me fiercely. I could feel his ribs beneath the light flannel shirt he wore and it made a lump rise up in my throat. To think that this lovely, warm, intelligent human being was wasting away made me sad beyond reason. I had to fight to hold back the tears.

I turned and walked briskly away, marveling at the way my emotions seemed to get the better of me these days. For years, I'd managed to keep all feelings at a safe distance, and my life was calm and orderly. Now it seemed there was no end to the depth and range of the emotions that threatened to overwhelm me at the slightest provocation. I was a sitting duck, and the gods and goddesses knew it.

Chapter Nineteen

He was getting restless. He knew it was still too soon, but he couldn't help it. He needed a little relief, and he needed it fast.

He could head on south, maybe to Bandon. The problem was, there was one he wanted right here in Kings Harbor. He knew this was a big mistake, and he'd been punishing himself for even thinking about it. But still, he couldn't quit thinking about it. She had that uppity, self-assured, almost condescending attitude that made him want to rip her nipples off.

Face it, he told himself, this one turns you on. He allowed himself the littlest smile, and quickly tucked it back where no one could see it. He'd just have to bide his time and keep things under control. But even so, he was picturing the things he'd do to her and he shuddered.

Chapter Twenty

"You cuddled with any coeds yet?" Martha asked when she came on the line.

"Very funny, Harper. For your information, I've got some actual news, if you're the slightest bit interested."

Martha's chuckle ended mid-laugh. "Hit me," she said, all business.

"Last night I had a date with the boy Lisa Lane was with the night she took her fatal swim. And guess what? He slipped me a Mickey. Actually, I'd bet money it was a roofie. Not only that, but he chased me through ten thousand miles of sand dunes before trying to track me down in his truck."

"You sure he wasn't just trying to see if you needed help or something?"

I didn't dare answer. I let the silence hang between us.

"Okay, okay," she said. "I stand corrected. So you think this bozo offed Lisa? If I recall, he's one of those tall, dark, handsome guys who gets a hard-on every time he looks in the mirror. Mikey something?"

"Markie Lewis. And yeah, that's him. But that's just the tip of the iceberg." As succinctly as I could, I recounted the details of the evening before, ending with Mary Jane's and Bridget's description of Brad Capers' unusual postcoital habit.

"Back that up and tell me again," Martha said. Her voice had gone cold.

"He ties up the end of his condoms, saving the semen inside and heaves them as far as he can, shouting 'Bombs away!' "

"And this is always in the dunes?"

"Well, hell, Martha. For all I know he does the same thing in Motel Sixes. But he's done it in the dunes at least a couple of times. I've got two eyewitnesses."

"Jesus H. Christ," Martha muttered. I hadn't heard that tone of voice from her in a long time and it scared me. She went on. "I haven't had a chance to tell you yet, but the DNA test came back from those condoms. Guess what? The stuff inside the last condom doesn't match the semen in the first two. Our first thought was that maybe we've got a copycat killer. Then we start thinking, could the killer be gay? Gets his lovers to leave their rubbers behind, then uses those? And the one thing that's been driving everyone crazy is the sand. And now you tell me this Brad what's-his-name ties his condoms in little balls like our killer and tosses them into the dunes, shouting 'Bombs Away.' I'm not sure what this means, but I sure as hell intend to find out."

"You think Brad is the serial killer?"

"Possibly. It still doesn't explain the third condom having a different semen type than the first two."

"Unless he's not the only one who does it. His best friend happens to be Markie Lewis." I let that sink in.

"The one who slipped you a roofie." It wasn't a question.

"The same drug they found in Lisa Lane's body. Did any of the murder victims have Rohypnol in their systems?" My palms felt sweaty on the receiver.

"No. All three had traces of chloroform in their lungs, though. We figure he knocks them out long enough to get them into his vehicle."

"Could there be two killers, Martha? Is that a possibility?"

"It's possible, but not likely, Cass. I see this guy working alone. What's your take on this Brad Capers?"

"He's a blond, surfer-type. Talks through his nose like he's trying not to exhale. Like he's just taken a big toke. Basically a real jerk. Yesterday I saw him belittle a cast member who has a speech impediment, and the orchestra conductor had to chastise him for harassing the female lead. The fact that his best friend happens to be Markie Lewis is all the character reference either one of them deserves. A friendship made in hell. Although half the women on campus seem to be smitten with one or the other."

"You know what kind of vehicle he drives?"

"No, but I can find out. Markie Lewis drives a black Chevy truck, if that helps. And, yes, it has four-wheel drive. He bragged about it last night."

"Listen, Cass. You've done more than I'd ever hoped for. I've got enough now to convince Grimes to let Langly back in on this, and I'd like to check out both these jokers myself, before I break the news about the condoms to the

Feds. It's probably best if you just unenroll yourself and slip back to Rainbow Lake. No point in pushing your luck."

"Actually, Martha, I've got a little unfinished business here. And as long as I'm hanging around, I may as well keep my eyes and ears open.

"Listen, just be careful, Cass. I mean it. Don't go trying to be heroic on me. If either of these clowns *is* involved, you could find yourself in danger. Let me take it from here."

She made me cross my heart and hope to die before she'd let me hang up.

I dreaded doing what came next, but I couldn't avoid it any longer. I waited nervously outside Rhonda Lou Whittaker's door, the paper bag clutched nervously in one hand. I knew I could've just waited until she left again and then snuck back in to replace the diaries, but she deserved better. When she opened the door, I was starting to regret this decision.

"Cassidy! What a surprise. Come on in. I was just making coffee."

I followed her into the house and dropped the bag on the coffee table.

"What's that?" she asked, her brown eyes narrowed suspiciously. I could see her mind working as she moved toward the bag.

"There's something I need to tell you," I said, blocking her path. "Go ahead and get the coffee. This could take a while."

When she came back in, she looked nervous, the way someone expecting bad news does. She set my cup on the table and sat down across from me.

"I'm not really a student."

"Okay." She knew there was more and waited me out.

"I'm a private investigator, and a friend of mine, a cop, asked me to look into Lisa's death, because she wasn't a hundred percent convinced that the death was accidental, but her boss has closed the case. So I'm undercover as a college student, trying to see if I can find anything that the cops missed."

"You don't really need the townhouse," she said. It wasn't a question. Just confirmation of more bad news.

"No, but if I did, you'd be my first choice as a roommate." I tried a smile.

"Yeah, right. Just tell me this. Was that you who broke into my house that night? I mean, were you just pretending to have seen someone?" She looked like she might cry any minute.

"No, that wasn't me. I really did see someone, which made me wonder what it was they were after. You were acting sort of secretive, which made me think you knew what they had come for. And you didn't seem all that worried about it, which led me to believe that you not only knew what it was but exactly where it was." I took a breath and went on. "Earlier, when I'd asked you whether Lisa kept a diary, I thought you evaded the question. I just put two and two together. When her bookshelves were ransacked, it seemed possible the intruder was looking for the diary. I didn't think you'd admit to taking it, but I thought the diary might hold some evidence that could help the investigation."

"And did you think *my* diary might help the investigation too?" She looked pointedly at the bag on the table. "Or was that just an added bonus, getting to read through someone else's private thoughts?" Her stare pinned me down with anger.

"I'm sorry," I said lamely. "I really am. You have every right to hate me. Sometimes there are aspects of my job that I don't like. I don't know what else to say."

"Correct me if I'm wrong, but isn't breaking and entering still against the law, even for private investigators? Isn't taking someone's private property still theft? I mean, did I miss a big law change or something? What you may consider distasteful aspects of your job, others might consider criminal acts."

"You're right," I admitted. "You could call the cops right now and press charges. At the very least, I'd lose my license."

"Why'd you bring them back?" she asked, finally taking the diaries from their bag. "You could've just trashed them. Or left them anonymously on the doorstep. I never would've thought it was you."

"The thought never crossed my mind," I lied. "I may break the law every now and then, but down deep I'm basically a decent person."

We both sipped coffee while she thought about this. Finally, she exhaled heavily. "So, did you find anything helpful? In either diary?"

I sighed with relief. For a while there, I'd been afraid she might actually call the cops. "I wish I had. I can't figure out why anyone would break into Lisa's room to read her diary, unless they were afraid of what she might have written. There was nothing in what she did write that seemed the least bit incriminating."

"It wasn't her diary they were after," Rhonda said calmly. "I thought at first it might be, but then when I noticed they'd been in my darkroom, I figured it out."

"What do you mean? What was it?"

"She borrowed my camera that night. Not my good one. Just an old thirty-five-millimeter Instamatic. She'd been taking pictures all week. That's how Lisa was. She'd get obsessed with an idea and do nothing else for a while, until a new interest caught her attention, and then she'd drop the old one just like that. I figured the camera obsession had at least a week to go before she discovered something else."

"And where is this camera?" I asked, feeling my pulse quicken.

Rhonda shrugged. "I asked a couple of her friends, you know, once I thought about it. I mean, at first, it was the last thing on my mind. But even though they remember seeing her with it that night, no one seems to know what happened to it. The police never said a word about it either. My guess is, someone stole it."

I knew that the only reason someone would break into Lisa's room to get the camera was if she'd taken a picture of something they didn't want anyone else to see.

"I feel like everyone and their brother has been in my house the last couple of days," Rhonda said, shaking her head.

"I'm really sorry," I said again. It was inadequate and I knew it, but this time, she offered me a small smile.

"I'm just sorry you're not really going to be my roommate. I was looking forward to it."

"Listen, for what it's worth, I'm still undercover, at least for a while. Can we just let this be our secret for now?"

"Well, seeing as you now know all of mine, I guess it's only fair I should know one of yours." This time, her smile was genuine. "Keep me informed, okay? She may have had her faults, but she was still my roommate. I'd like to know what really happened."

"Deal," I said. I stood up and we shook on it. It didn't seem silly at all.

Chapter Twenty-one

   With the play due to open in just over a week, I knew the whole cast would be putting in extra hours. I hadn't yet figured out the best way to deal with Markie Lewis, but I needed to find out what he knew about Lisa's missing camera. Besides, I still wanted to confront him about the roofies. I knew that what Martha had said about sicko-psycho types working solo was probably true, and as much as I despised Markie Lewis, deep down I couldn't quite picture him as a serial killer. On the other hand, I did think there was more to Lisa's death than met the eye, and the missing camera might just be the key. Like it or not, I was going to have to talk to the S.O.B. again.

I left Rhonda's apartment and headed straight for the theater. It was close to eleven, just about time for a break. The first person I saw was Rita Colby, smoking a clove cigarette next to the coffee machine where I'd first met her.

"Have a good time?" she asked, her pupils mere slits against the overcast day. It had finally quit raining, but the day was no less dismal because of it.

"No, actually. I had a really horrible time. Someone drugged me and I think it was your pal Markie. After what you told me, I don't have many doubts about what he had in mind. I just wonder if that's what happened with Lisa Lane too."

"You're joking, right? He really drugged you? That fucking cretin! I can't believe he'd do that, two weeks after Lisa's death!" Rita's eyes burned with pure venom.

"Know where he is? I'd sure like to chat with him, now that I'm sober."

"Well, since I just saw Brad get something out of his bus and rush toward the restroom ten minutes ago, my guess is they're snorting coke in the bathroom. If you don't mind, I'd like to hear this myself." She stepped on what was left of the cigarette and led me around to the back of the theater.

"What kind of bus?" I asked.

"It's that old VW camper van by my Honda. The brown one." She pointed back toward the lot and I saw it. It was one of the vehicles I'd counted the day before. We stepped up a short ramp and entered a door I'd not noticed before.

"Men's restroom," she said. "They hang out in here on breaks."

She pushed open the door and I was aware of a sudden *whoosh* I couldn't quite identify in the dark. Then

I realized I was hearing the sudden collective intake of breath and subsequent lack of movement. They were holding their breath, probably trying to figure out if they should be flushing stuff down the toilet.

As my eyes adjusted to the darkened room, I made out Markie's silhouette, leaning over the counter, a rolled-up bill a half-inch from his nose. He was frozen like that, and I had a tremendous urge to make him sneeze. The small pile of white powder would have floated harmlessly into the sink, and I'd have loved rushing to turn on the tap. Instead, I turned on the lights.

"Wha' the fuck you doin' in here?" Brad Capers demanded, squinting against the sudden glare. "Get the fuck out." His blond, surfer hair was pulled back in a leather thong and he looked most Biblical in his white robe and leather sandals, a strange contrast to the harsh words. I felt the hairs on the back of my neck prickle.

"If you need to snort that, go ahead," I said to Markie. "But then I need to see you outside. I'll give you thirty seconds."

I turned to leave, with Rita right on my heels. We both heard Brad shout after us, "Or what?" But we ignored him, and before we could even reach the stand of trees across from the bathroom, Mark Lewis came barreling out.

"Shit, Cassidy. What happened to you? I was worried sick!"

"Really?" I intoned. "When was that? Before or after you decided to drug me with Rohypnol?"

"Huh?"

"Roofies," I said. I watched his pupils bleed into his irises, making huge globes in the centers of his shiny eyes. It made it difficult to read him.

"Oh shit," he said at last. "I figured that's what had happened. You musta got my beer. Damn. I thought I'd gotten a bum steer when I didn't feel nothin' happening. But then Mary Jane said you were sick and all, and when I went to find you, you just took off. I thought something

146

bad had happened. I kept calling and calling but you wouldn't even turn around. I even went looking for you in my truck — you can ask anyone. After what happened with Lisa and all, you know, I was pretty freaked out. Why'd you run off like that, anyway?" His tanned, handsome face regarded me innocently, but I still felt prickly hairs running up my forearms.

"Because," Rita interjected, "she's obviously smarter than I was. Or Lisa, for that matter. And if you think the police are going to buy your bullshit about her getting your laced beer, you're more of an idiot than I thought."

"Shut up, Rita," Markie spat. "For your information I really cared about Lisa. And I didn't need no roofie."

"Then why did the police find Rohypnol in her system the night she died?" I asked. Both of them turned to stare at me and I realized I may have blown my cover.

"She wanted to take one!" Markie said. "Lots of people do. You can't blame that on me!"

"I suppose you tell people I wanted one too?" Rita said, taking a step toward Markie. The coke in his system was making his left foot tap to some unheard tempo. His pupil-less eyes were glassy.

"I thought it would relax you," he said. "You were always so uptight. You know. I didn't think you'd take one if I offered it, but I thought you'd like it once you experienced it. And you did, Rita. Tell me you didn't have fun that night. Ask anyone, that was the funnest you've ever been!"

"My goal in life, Markie, is not to be fun for other people. What you did was criminal. Among other things, it's called rape. If I'd had my shit together as much then as I do now, I'd have pressed charges. In fact, the more I think of it, I still might."

Markie blinked slowly, his long black lashes waving in slow motion while he tried to process this startling bad news. "It'd be your word against mine," he said at last. His full red lips parted softly, giving the hint of a smile.

147

"Like it would've been Lisa's word against yours?" I asked. Markie looked at me blankly. "Everyone knows you had sex that night, Markie. And you could probably deny it and get away with it, if it weren't for the pictures." This time, the pupils popped into action and his whole face went rigid. Bingo, I thought.

"What pictures?" he asked, too late. Even Rita was smiling, but then, she didn't know I was bluffing.

"Oh, don't be obtuse, Markie. You know damn well what pictures. And I have half a mind to turn them over to the police. Give me one reason why I shouldn't."

"Because they're private!" he shouted.

If there was such a thing as double Bingo, I'd just hit it. I couldn't help myself, I started to chuckle.

"You fucking bitch," he said under his breath. Just like that his eyes had gone from scared to scary. He took a step toward me, his massive arms suddenly bunched into muscle.

"Is he bothering you, young lady?" I turned to see Mr. Purvis stepping around the corner. Like always, he was dressed in a black suit, with a crisp white shirt and narrow tie. His old-fashioned glasses had slid down his nose, giving his homely face a matronly air and his red hair stood out against his porcelain skin, contrasting sharply with Markie's dark scowling countenance. "I'm ashamed of you," he said to Markie, his voice low and controlled. "We'll have a word about this later. Right now, I want you back onstage where you belong. The entire cast has been held up by your absence."

Markie stomped off, and Rita shot me a grin. "I better get back too," she said. "But we need to talk later." She smiled and punched me in the arm. "I knew I liked you." She rushed off, leaving me alone with Mr. Purvis.

He reached out and lightly patted my shoulder. "You shouldn't take these boys too seriously," he said. "They're at that age. You know, girls mature so much faster than boys, and yet, when boys do mature a little bit, they suddenly think they're men. I'm afraid Mr. Lewis has fallen into that category." He let out a chuckle, suddenly embarrassed by his speech. He smoothed his wiry orange hair back from his forehead. "Well, I'd best be getting back. But if Markie gives you any more trouble, you just let me know. I don't like to see improper behavior in any of my young men."

I watched him stride back toward the theater with his odd gait, like someone whose legs weren't quite in agreement about which way they wanted to go. It made his head bob, and he reminded me somewhat of a penguin.

As soon as he left, I knew what I wanted to do. I rushed to the now familiar phone booth and searched the pages for Corey Monroe. He answered on the third ring.

"Corey. It's Cassidy. The doughnut fiend. Do you by any chance have Gracie's phone number? Or last name? I need to reach her right away."

"It's Cassidy," Corey said to someone else, his hand over the receiver. "She wants your phone number. Hang on a sec," he said to me.

A moment later, Gracie's strong, clear voice came over the line. "You feeling better?" she asked.

"Yes. But not as good as I'll feel if you can help me do something. Is there any chance you can spare an hour or so sometime today?"

"Is now good?"

"Now is perfect." I told her where I was and hung up smiling. Lauren Monroe might be the most confused, infuriating woman I'd ever met, but her brother and Gracie were turning out to be real finds.

Gracie pulled up in an old battered red truck that looked vintage 1950s. She was wearing a white ribbed muscle shirt under a denim workshirt tucked into faded Levi's. Her Nikes were easily a size ten.

"I hope I didn't interrupt anything too important," I said, climbing in beside her. "Turn left here." I'd seen Markie's truck parked in the lot across from the theater and had Gracie pull up behind it.

"Nah. I was just giving Corey a massage. Acutally, we'd finished. We were sitting around shootin' the breeze."

"You're a masseuse?" I asked.

"Among other things. I practice the healing arts. Also the martial arts. I also play a mean banjo and can line-dance your ass off. A woman of many talents." She smiled and let her gray eyes settle on mine. "Which talent were you requiring?" she finally asked.

"Your size." I laughed, hoping she wouldn't be offended. To my relief she grinned. So I told her what I wanted. Which also required my telling her who I really was and what I was doing. It took a while, but she listened patiently, nodding without interrupting.

"I knew Corey knew something," she said finally. "He was grinning like a Cheshire cat when he asked me what I thought of you. That little booger."

"I swore him to secrecy," I said. "It's important Lauren doesn't know my true identity. She might unwittingly tip my hand and I can't afford for her to do that just yet." Again, Gracie nodded.

Just then, Markie's well-muscled frame rounded the corner and he sauntered toward his truck. The initial rush of coke must have been wearing off because his motions were less jerky than they were earlier, and he was back to the loose shambling gait of a growing boy with the world in his hip pocket.

"Now?" Gracie asked, cracking her knuckles.

"Now," I answered. I slid out of the passenger's door and the two of us moved in on Markie before he even saw us.

"What?" he said, eyeing me with contempt. He was already climbing into his truck and I slid in right behind him, pushing him over before he could protest. Gracie

150

slipped into the passenger's side and we both locked the doors, sandwiching him between us on the front seat.

"Hey!" he shouted. Poor Markie had been reduced to monosyllabic intonations. I turned on the ignition. He reached over to grab the keys and Gracie put her left hand on the back of his neck. I'm not sure what she did, but he immediately slumped back against the seat and let out a pathetic groan.

"Blackbelt," she explained simply.

"Okay, okay," he moaned. I pulled away from the curb and headed toward the dunes.

"This is kidnapping," he said feebly.

Gracie cracked her knuckles and he shut up. I did my best to suppress a grin and we rode the rest of the way in silence.

"What's this all about?" he tried again, once I'd parked the truck. I was as close as I could remember to where we'd been the night before.

"This is your big chance," I said. "We're going to reenact a scene. You get to be the star. Two stars, actually."

I hopped down from the truck and Markie followed. I was pretty sure Gracie's presence had something to do with his sudden, eager compliance.

"I don't get it," he said. I looked into his big, dark eyes and saw true bewilderment. Also, a little fear.

"I want to know what happened with Lisa, Markie. I want to know every detail."

His shoulders slumped forward. "I already told the police everything. I don't gotta tell you nothing!"

Gracie stretched her fingers nonchalantly and Markie glanced her way.

"Take me to where you last saw her, Markie. Oh, by the way, this is Gracie. I brought her with me because, although I'm pretty good at telling when someone is lying, Gracie is something of an expert. You're such a good liar, Markie, I figured I'd need an expert."

Gracie flashed him a grin.

"I never lied about nothin'." He eyed Gracie the second he said it. She shook her head once, slowly, like a Doberman issuing a silent warning. Markie actually shuddered, then started up the dune in front of us.

My legs were in much worse shape than they'd been the night before, but I was pumped with adrenaline, which made the trek seem shorter.

"Is this what you wanted?" he asked, breathing heavily. We were standing in the middle of unending dunes, with thatches of Douglas fir and spruce dotting the vast whiteness around us. Even without the tent, I sort of recognized the place. The firepit was the only physical evidence of the party, though. All footprints had been swept away by the rain and wind.

"You and Lisa went off to be alone," I said. "Show me where."

"Are you weird, or what?" he asked.

"Or what," I said. "Show me." His black gaze was intended to make me wither. When it didn't work, he led the way.

"We came here," he said, stopping beneath a stand of Douglas fir. He had his hands on his hips and his eyes were furious. "So what?"

"So tell me, Markie. Everything. Every little detail. What you did. What she did. Like that."

"Jesus, this is sick. What are you, a homo?"

"Yeah," I said. "Got a problem with that?" He looked from me to Gracie and his face went red. "Start talking."

"Fuck off." He pushed past me and started back down the dune. As quick as a cat, Gracie moved behind him. Her left foot tripped him up and he fell forward into her right fist, which caught him in the throat. When he whirled around, one chop dropped him to his knees.

He was gasping as Gracie helped him to his feet. "I believe she asked you a question, son."

Markie struggled to recapture his breath. "Honest, she wanted it as much as I did. More, even!"

I stared at him, hard.

"What? You want details? Okay. We sort of undressed each other over there and then she chased me to right here and then we, you know, fell to the ground here, and we did it. You want a blow-by-blow, or is that good enough?"

"He's leaving something out," Gracie said, taking a step toward him. I started to answer, but Markie interrupted.

"Okay! Look, as far as I was concerned it was over, but Lisa started taking pictures, saying she wanted to 'capture the moment.' Well, shit, I was naked. She'd had this stupid camera for days and she kept clicking away like she was some damned photographer for *People* magazine or something. Which was okay, I guess, except this was different. I told her to stop and she wouldn't. Then I got mad, and then she got mad, and that's when she went off into the dunes. That was the last I saw of her, I swear. I went back to the fire, and when she didn't follow, I figured, screw her. Later, I did go back, but she was long gone. That's all I know."

He was silent, looking down at the breakers. Gracie and I exchanged glances.

"What did she take pictures of that made you so mad, Markie?" I asked.

"I already told you! I was naked!"

"You said she went into the dunes. What'd you do? Toss her camera? Did she run off to retrieve it? No one runs off into the dunes for no reason, Markie." His eyes grew round and I felt a small thrill of victory. It wasn't a ringer, but I was pretty sure I'd struck metal.

"Son, I'm giving you one chance to tell this lady the truth," Gracie said. She stepped forward and laid one hand on Markie's shoulder. His face went white.

"It's personal," he said, his voice suddenly small.

"So is murder," I said.

"Oh, Jesus. Is that what you think? I swear on my grandmother's grave, I had nothing to do with Lisa's death. Look. It's embarrassing, okay? After we, uh, you know, had sex, I, uh, sort of tossed the rubber, and Lisa wanted to retrieve it. I mean, she took pictures of me throwing it, and then she went after it. Said that could be our first child, or some such shit. That's when I left. I just figured she'd follow."

My head had started to throb.

"You tied your condom like a balloon and heaved it into the dunes?" My voice was wavery. Markie just glared at me. "How many of you do this?" I asked, my voice coming back.

"Answer her, son." Gracie tightened her grip on Markie's shoulder.

"Just me and Brad. It's kind of a private joke, that's all. Like a million years from now, when the aliens land on earth and human life is extinct, they'll find our rubbers and our sperm will still be good, you know, and we'll be the new fathers of the land. Like, our sperm will be the only thing that saves mankind."

Gracie and I looked at each other and neither of us laughed. "What else?" I said.

"Nothing, I swear. That's it!"

I looked at Gracie and she nodded. The shithead might just be telling the truth. Gracie took her hand off his shoulder and Markie relaxed considerably. He even managed to swagger.

"Show me," I said suddenly.

"What?"

"I'll bet ten bucks you've got some cherry-flavored condoms in your back pocket. Take one out."

Markie's face went white again.

"Do it," Gracie said.

He did.

"I want to see you do it," I said. Now his face went pink and he looked panic-stricken. "Don't flatter yourself," I said. "Just fill the damn thing with sand until the weight feels about right. Then tie it and heave it. The same as you did that night."

"You're crazy!" he said. But the look of relief on his face was comical. He kneeled and started stuffing sand into the condom. It took an eternity.

"Make sure you get the weight right," I said.

"Jesus. It's not like I weigh the damn things."

"Close your eyes and try to remember."

To my surprise, he did. Finally, he tied the end of the condom and looked at me expectantly.

"Do it just like that night. Right down to the 'Bombs Away!' "

"How the fuck did you know that?" he demanded, his eyes wide.

"Just do it," I said.

Markie got on all fours and held the condom in his right hand. He closed his eyes, whether mustering courage or just reenacting the scene, I couldn't tell. Then he rolled to his left, cocked his right arm and shouted the ridiculous "Bombs Away!" The sand-filled condom sailed through the air and disappeared over the crest of a dune.

"Satisfied?" he asked, standing up to brush the sand from his knees and hands. He was actually looking satisfied with himself. Cocky even. His black eyes glistened.

"Not quite," I said. "This is for last night." I pulled back and let my right fist rocket straight into his stomach. He immediately doubled over, gasping. "And this is for Rita Colby." I caught his chin with an upper left that sent him toppling backwards. He scrambled to his feet and started to charge me, his black eyes suffused with red.

"You fucking bitch!" he screamed. He dove at me, trying to knock me to the ground, but I was ready for him. I stepped to the left and as he flew toward me, I performed the one really wicked karate kick I had perfected, a swift blow to the balls. He toppled like a felled tree and lay whimpering on the ground.

"That was for Lisa Lane," I said. "I'll leave your truck where I found it on campus." I held his keys between my thumb and forefinger and dangled them, just in case he didn't get it.

He may have thought about following us but it never happened. Gracie and I stomped through the sand in the direction of his hand-launched condom, neither of us saying a word.

"Damn, girl," she finally muttered, breaking the silence. "What the hell did you need me for?"

"Moral support," I said. "Besides, this will take two of us."

"What exactly are we looking for?" she asked, still chuckling.

"A thirty-five-millimeter Instamatic. And I hope we find it before whoever else is looking for it does."

We found Markie's sand-filled condom with relative ease. It helped that it was bright cherry red. From there, we began a methodical search, each working our own designated sections. A rake would've been nice, but I hadn't thought that far ahead. We used our hands and feet. It had been two weeks, enough time for the wind and rain to erase any prints. Enough time to bury a little camera. After thirty minutes we were both exhausted and I called it quits.

"His throw could've been off," Gracie said, trudging across the dune toward me. She was breathing as heavily as I was.

"I'll leave something here to mark the spot," I said, looking around. "I'll bring Martha here tomorrow, if I can get hold of her. Maybe a couple of rakes would help."

Gracie took off her denim shirt, revealing finely muscled arms the color of dark honey. "Use this," she offered. "I'm too hot anyway."

I buried one sleeve in the sand to keep it from blowing

away and we trudged on back toward the road, hoping Markie hadn't managed to hotwire the truck. Neither of us wanted to add more miles to our outing.

We were almost to the road when Gracie stopped and grabbed my arm. "Be still my heart," she said.

"What?"

"Over there. Tell me that's not what I think it is." She pointed to the unmistakable black strip of nylon that served as a neck strap for a camera. It stuck out of the sand by only a few inches. Another day, another windy storm, the strap would've been completely covered.

I dug the camera out of the sand and cradled it in my hands, afraid of what the wind and sand and rain and sun had done to the film. Then Gracie and I raced each other back to Markie's truck, whooping and hollering like two schoolgirls. Neither of us spent much time worrying about where Markie was or about how mad we might have made him. All either of us could think of was the fastest way to get the film developed.

Chapter Twenty-two

Rhonda took one look at Gracie and me and headed straight for the darkroom.

"How long will it take?" I asked.

"Not long. Just make yourselves at home and I'll be out as soon as I'm finished. Fix yourselves something to drink. And don't worry. I haven't botched a roll of film in a long time." When she saw the worried look on my face she laughed. "Relax. I'm actually pretty good at this." With that, she disappeared into the darkroom.

Gracie took Rhonda at her word and began searching through the refrigerator for something to drink. I dialed Martha's number at work and got her voice mail.

"Martha, it's me. Guess what? I was right. Brad Capers isn't the only condom-tossing weirdo around here. His buddy Markie Lewis does the same thing. He swears they're the only two. It's sort of a private joke with them. After having sex with Lisa Lane on the night she died, he apparently tossed the condom into the dunes. They got into a fight and she went off by herself in the same direction. For some reason, she wanted the condom back." I took a breath. "Anyway, she had a camera with her when she left. Markie says he never saw her again, and he might be telling the truth, I don't know. I do know Brad Capers was out there somewhere with Mary Jane around that time. Could be Lisa Lane snapped a picture or two of them and Brad didn't like it. My guess is that she took a picture of something someone didn't like. Anyway, I managed to find the camera and I'm getting the film developed right now. Thank God it's black-and-white film. We should know within the hour. I'll let you know."

When I hung up Gracie came back into the living room.

"All she's got is diet stuff. Coke okay?"

I nodded, and she handed me a can. The two of us began pacing the little living room.

"So, Corey tells me things didn't go so hot last night after I left. What happened?" She regarded me with raised eyebrows.

"I blew it, that's what happened. I sort of came on to her. I mean, I thought she was coming on to me. I made a fool of myself, is what happened."

By now Gracie was chuckling. "Poor, poor Lauren. I've never known anyone with worse romantic luck than her. She's practically convinced herself to live a celibate life after the last disaster, and then here you come along and she sees it all happening again."

"What exactly happened that was so bad?" I asked.

"Didn't Corey tell you? Lauren broke a cardinal rule and it cost her dearly. She fell in love with a student.

159

True, it was a grad student. She wasn't exactly robbing the cradle. But still, there's a code of ethics that says teachers don't sleep with their students. Lauren broke that rule. And eventually the student broke her heart. She didn't just come out here to be with Corey, you know. She came out here to get away from Stanford."

"So she is gay? Please tell me this student was a woman. I've been going crazy trying to figure her out."

"Yes, the student was definitely a woman. And Lauren Monroe is the furthest thing from being homophobic there is. What she is afraid of is students. It isn't your gayness that has her running scared. It's her reaction to you and the fact that she thinks she's falling for another student. I can't wait to tell her you're a private investigator. I'd pay to see the look on her face."

My insides had begun to do ridiculous somersaults at this news. But her next question brought a sudden lump to my throat.

"You're not going to break her heart, are you?"

I looked at Gracie and we both stopped pacing. Her gray eyes appraised me and I found it difficult to answer. "I hope not," I said truthfully. "I'm not sure I have any business even pursuing her at this point. I'm just acting on impulse. I'm not really letting myself think too much about it."

Gracie raised an eyebrow. "There's someone else?"

I sipped my Coke, hoping it would help with the sudden difficulty I was having swallowing. "Her name is Maggie Carradine," I found myself saying. "We've been together for a couple of years. Except, four months ago she left. Not just me. She left her house, her patients, everything, so that she could fly off to France to be with her ex-lover who's dying of cancer." I inhaled deeply. "Maggie must have quite a therapeutic effect on the woman. She's feeling so much better they've decided to go on vacation to Switzerland." I couldn't keep the sarcasm out of my voice.

160

"It must be hard on you," she said.

I stared out Rhonda's window, not wanting Gracie to see the tears that had sprung up out of nowhere. "I guess I'm still in shock. I thought Maggie and I had something special," I admitted. "How many times can a person find love? I really thought Maggie was it. Now it looks like it was a one-way commitment. Even when she told me not to wait for her, I thought she'd be back. I mean, going off to help her ex-lover was one thing. But it's turned into something else. So, no, to answer your question, I guess there really isn't anyone else."

To my surprise, Gracie slipped her arm around my shoulders and pulled me to her. She was a good foot taller than me, and my head rested against her breast.

"Rebound affairs don't usually work out," she said. I nodded, trying not to let my emotions get the better of me. Somehow, this big, muscled amazon had an amazing gift for empathy that reduced me to Jell-O. "But every now and then they do," she said. I looked at her and she flashed me a lopsided grin. "Me and Doreen, we got together before her ex had even left the house. And we've been together twelve years now. You just never know, Cassidy. The thing about love is, if you can love once, you can love again. I don't think there's any limit on it. It's not like God allots everyone so many chances, and that's it. Sometimes you've just got to find love where it is."

"I don't want to make another mistake," I said.

"Who said you made one?" Her gray eyes bore into mine. "You think there's some guarantee? I know so many people who won't fly in planes, or ride roller-coasters or hike mountains, and all because they're afraid they might die. Well, of course they're going to die. We all are. But their fear of death is robbing them of life. The only mistake you can make is by not loving when you have the chance. By not living the life you've got."

I looked at her and her chiseled cheeks darkened.

"Forgive me, sometimes I go off like that. I can't help

it. It's my Cherokee heritage. Every now and then I sound just like my great-grandmother. She used to bore everyone to tears with her sage pontifications."

"I'm not bored yet," I said, smiling. "So you're saying I should quit feeling guilty about these feelings I have for Lauren and just let nature take its course? I should just forget about Maggie?"

"Did I say that?" she asked, looking innocent. "I would never dream of giving advice on such important matters." She took a swig of her Coke. "I'm merely saying that fear should not be our motivating force. And so often guilt is nothing more than fear that someone will think less of us for doing something we really want to do. See? You've got me doing it again. If you don't stop me soon, I'll have to drag out my soapbox."

I laughed, feeling strangely refreshed and energized. Maybe it was the caffeine, I thought, looking at the Coke can in my hand. But I didn't think so. I was pretty sure Gracie had just shared with me another one of her many talents.

The door banged open from the darkroom and we both rushed to meet Rhonda coming toward us.

"Don't touch these," she warned, spreading the photos out on the coffee table. We crowded around the table and impatiently watched as she laid the still-damp photos in chronological order. "Talk about hung like a horse," she giggled, placing several pictures of the naked Markie Lewis in front of us. I couldn't tell if the anger in his eyes was feigned or real. He was shaking his finger at the camera, but I thought he might actually have enjoyed Lisa's taking his picture like that, right after sex.

But Lisa Lane's amateur skills had still managed to catch the look of triumph on his face as he cocked his arm back to heave the condom into the dunes. I was still studying his face when Rhonda placed the last two pictures on the table. I'm not sure if my heart actually stopped, but I know my breathing did. I felt all the color drain right out of my face.

"Who's that?" Gracie asked, pointing to the last pictures.

Lisa must have been crouched behind a sand dune, because the angle of the photo was close to the ground and the bottom third of the picture showed a closeup of sand granules. And while I couldn't make out the features, there was no mistaking the dark shape of a figure scurrying across the dunes. She'd gotten two shots. In the first one his back was to the camera, not twenty feet from where she lay. In the second, he was farther off, but turned toward her, and in the distance was the unmistakable outline of a dark, boxy van.

"Can you enlarge these?" I asked, my heart racing.

"Not with the equipment I have here," Rhonda said. "But it's doable. There's a place in town that has the right equipment, but they'd be closed by now. Who do you think that is?" She was holding the photo by the edges, peering at it closely.

"I have no idea," I said. But I did have an idea of what he was doing. And the hairs along the back of my neck were standing straight up.

I wrapped the photos carefully and put them in my pocket. Rhonda had already gone back into the darkroom to make second prints, promising to hide the negatives in the same place she'd hidden the diaries, in case someone came looking for them again. I told her my friend Martha Harper would be by to collect both the prints and negatives as soon as I could get in touch with her. I made her promise not to open the door for anyone else. The way her eyes twinkled, I could tell she was having the time of her life. It dawned on me that Rhonda Lou Whitaker would make a hell of a crime photographer.

After leaving another brief message on Martha's voice mail, I tried her at home and got Tina.

"Cassidy! Baby, how you doin'?"

"I'm doing fine, Tina. Martha's not there, by any chance?"

"I wish she were. You sound worried. What's up?"

"I need to get a message to her as soon as possible. I've left two messages on her voice mail, but I thought I'd leave one with you too. It's important."

"Just a second, let me grab a pen."

I gave Tina Rhonda's address, explaining about the photographs and the need to have two of them enlarged. I told her my theory about what the pictures meant.

"Is this for real, Cassidy? You think that girl got a picture of the serial killer? Collecting condoms?"

"I could be wrong," I said.

"You could be in danger," she said, her voice dropping an octave.

"No one knows I found the camera," I said. Except it occurred to me that Markie Lewis probably had a pretty good idea what Gracie and I had gone looking for. Would he dare tell anyone what we had done to him? I doubted it.

Tina promised to track down Martha and deliver the message for me and I thanked her.

Gracie was looking at me strangely. "You think this killer sits out in the dunes waiting for the boys to heave their condoms into the sand, and then he uses them to leave with the murder victims?" Her gray eyes were wide.

"You're not supposed to know about that," I said. "Please forget you heard that part of the conversation."

"Jesus," she said. "Then it could be true. The serial

killer may very well have also killed your Lisa Lane. Because he knew she'd seen him retrieving the condoms."

"Exactly," I said. "At least that's the way I'm starting to think. But why didn't he go back for the camera?"

"Maybe he did," she said. "Maybe he couldn't find it. You know how hard we looked. It was a total fluke I even saw that strap. If we'd gone in even a slightly different direction, we'd have missed it."

"And then, when he couldn't find it," I said, "maybe he thought someone else had picked it up. That's why he broke into Lisa's apartment. Hoping someone had returned it to her house."

"Come on. Let's get out of here," Gracie said. "I'm beginning to feel like I need a drink."

There wasn't much more I could do at the moment. As soon as Martha got my message, the case would be in her hands again. The police department would have no trouble getting the photos enlarged, and hopefully they'd be able to positively I.D. the van and person on the dunes.

I carefully zipped up the pocket that held the pictures and followed Gracie to her aging truck, thinking that a cold drink was exactly what the situation called for.

To my surprise, she pulled up in front of Lauren Monroe's apartment. I looked at her quizzically and she laughed.

"Don't worry, I'll protect you," she said, sliding out of the pickup.

"I wasn't exactly invited," I said. I was hesitant to go in.

"I happen to know that Lauren Monroe has the best wine collection this side of Napa Valley. And the price is definitely right. Besides, I think you two have some talking to do."

"I told you, Gracie. I can't afford to let Lauren know I'm working undercover until the case is closed. Some of the people in the play might be involved in this thing. We can't afford for her to tip my hand, even unwittingly."

"It seems to me, in light of what we've just discovered, the case is pretty much closed. I can't see either of those two boys rushing out to retrieve their own condoms, can you? I mean, you may not actually know who the killer is, but you can at least be fairly sure it isn't one of them. Right?"

"I'm not so sure. According to Mary Jane, Brad was with her that night while Lisa was with Markie. Later, people saw Brad and Markie together drinking beer. But there could be a time lapse in there. I don't know. I'm not comfortable ruling either of them out. For all I know, Brad's the killer, and steals Markie's condoms just to give the police false evidence." Still shaking my head, I followed Gracie to Lauren's door.

She was wearing a blue flannel shirt over soft worn Levi's and I couldn't help notice that the shirt's top buttons were open, revealing a tantalizing glimpse of cleavage. Her hair was down, blonde swirls around her shoulders, giving her a softened, vulnerable look. I found myself staring, at a sudden loss for words.

"Is the bar open? I'm buying," Gracie said, pushing her way past Lauren, who seemed as tongue-tied as I was.

"Of course. Come on in," she managed.

"How'd rehearsals go?" I asked lamely.

"Don't ask. It's been a nightmare. Everyone's fighting with everyone else backstage and it's coming through onstage." She ushered me in as she continued. "Mary Jane's not speaking to Brad, which is just terrific. It does wonders for the romance scenes. And Pontius Pilate has started to stutter onstage. Poor Roland. For some reason, he has no speech impediment at all when it comes to saying lines or singing, but he can't get a word out in real conversation. Now, this close to opening night, he starts stuttering onstage. It's terrible. Everyone else is trying to keep a straight face, but of course they can't. And then, to top it all off, your pal Markie decides to pass gas right in the middle of the grand finale. Jesus is standing there, tied to the cross and Judas passes gas. Naturally, Jesus starts laughing, and then all the Disciples join in and pretty soon even the orchestra is howling. Purvis threatened to quit if everyone didn't get back into character and replay the scene, but really, there was no point. I have to admit, even I had tears running down my face. I finally just went over and turned on the houselights and told them I'd see them all tomorrow. I couldn't take another minute of that madness."

I'd never heard the professor so talkative and there were little specks of color in her cheeks that I found very attractive.

"It sounds like you need this worse than we do," Gracie said, handing Lauren a glass of Chardonnay. I took one too and raised my glass in a toast.

"To opening night," I said.

"Please. Don't even mention that word. May it never arrive!" She raised her glass and swallowed deeply.

The wine was rich and smooth. I breathed it in and took another sip, savoring the complex, buttery flavor.

"So what have you two been up to that makes you in such need of liquid refreshment?" Lauren asked, folding herself onto the sofa. "Or dare I ask?"

"Cassidy has something she wants to tell you," Gracie said, avoiding the look I shot her. I could feel Lauren's gaze, like heat from a spotlight, warming my skin. I sat in the chair opposite them and tried not to squirm.

"There's no need to apologize, if that's what you're having so much trouble doing," Lauren said.

I hated to admit that I hadn't even thought about that. "Uh, well actually, there's something else," I said. I was having a terrible time getting the words out. For some reason, I felt like a kid who'd just gotten caught telling a big fib. I wasn't sure where to start.

"Cassidy's a private investigator working undercover," Gracie blurted.

I looked at her in amazement. "Well, that was subtle," I said.

"Jeez, you were never going to get it out. I just thought I'd help you get started." She turned to Lauren. "She's working on a big case and today we found something that might be really important. But it's her story. I should let her tell it." Gracie was clearly pleased with herself, but the look on Lauren's face told me she wasn't the least bit amused. Her eyes were ice.

"You're not a teaching assistant," she said. I shook my head. "You're not a student at all?" I shrugged, hoping she'd understand. "You didn't just spend however many years it was in Europe with your lover? You don't really speak French? You're not really planning on going to UCLA in the spring? Every single thing you told me was a lie?" Her tone was incredulous and she was clutching her glass so tightly, I was half-afraid she was going to hurl it at me.

"I was posing as a student so I could find out more about what happened to Lisa Lane," I started, but Lauren wasn't interested in hearing any more.

"Who else knows about this?" She was looking from me to Gracie, obviously hurt. "Does Corey know? Is that what you were telling him this morning?" I nodded, feeling trapped. If she'd just let me explain. But Lauren was already on her feet, headed for the door.

"Lauren," I started.

"Please not now, Cass. I've had enough surprises for one day."

She flung open the door and stood aside, obviously waiting for me to leave. I took one last, reluctant swallow of my wine and stood up.

"I'm sorry for misleading you," I said, but the door closed behind me before I could get another word out.

It was possible that Lauren Monroe was one of the most frustrating women I'd ever met, I thought. And also one of the most attractive. I walked down the sidewalk in the growing dusk, as confused about my own feelings as Lauren seemed about hers.

Even the thought of Mama Mangione's manicotti didn't cheer me. What I really needed was the comfort of my two cats. But I couldn't go home just yet. Not until Martha got my message and had a chance to study those photographs. Maybe I should just go back to Rhonda's and wait there. I was still debating this when a voice behind me took me by such surprise that I jumped. When I whirled around, my heart was actually pounding.

"Con-con-gratulations," Roland said, his cherubic cheeks glowing. Even in street clothes he resembled Julius Caesar, with his brown bangs cut straight across his forehead. His pudgy fingers tugged at his shirttail nervously.

"Roland. I didn't hear you come up. You practically scared me to death. Congratulations for what?"

"For ki-kicking the shit out of Ma-Ma-Markie Lewis. I wish I could have see-seen it." His watery blue eyes beamed as he spoke.

"How on earth did you hear about that?" I'd been banking on Markie's keeping his mouth shut.

"I was in the ba-bathroom at the Pizzaria and oh-oh-overheard him telling Brad Capers. They're planning to ge-get ee-even." His stuttering seemed even more pronounced than it had before, and it was painful to listen to him labor.

"Oh really? How's that?"

"Ma-Markie said he know-knows where you live. He said he wanted to ee-ee-even the score. And get some pictures too."

"You heard all this in the bathroom?"

He nodded, his eyes practically dancing with glee. "I

held my feet up. They didn't ee-ee-even know I was in there."

"Well, aren't you clever, Roland. Did they say anything else?"

Roland looked down at his feet and his cheeks turned pink. "He called you a dy-dy-dy . . ." He looked up helplessly.

"A dyke?" I asked. He nodded, clearly embarrassed. "What else?" I asked.

"He told B-Brad that Lisa Lane had ta-taken some pictures of him na-naked and that he thought you and your f-friend went looking for them. He wants them back."

"Roland, I really appreciate your telling me all this. Thanks for the warning."

"That's all right," he said, toeing the ground. "Everyone th-thinks what you did was pretty fu-funny."

My heart sank when he said this. "Everyone? You told others?"

"No, no, not me. Mary Jane. I just told her. Sh-she told the whole room. Even Mr. Purvis laughed. I think people are ti-ti-tired of Markie Lewis."

"What did Markie do?" I asked, feeling like things were spinning out of my control.

"He and Brad were already g-gone. They might have g-gone to your house. Did you find the pi-pictures that Lisa took?"

"Now what makes you ask that?"

Roland looked down quickly, as if he'd been caught doing something wrong. "I ju-ju-just wondered," he stammered. "No reason."

"You liked Lisa, didn't you, Roland?" I had no real idea why I was asking this. It just popped out.

"Oh, yes. She was real pre-pretty. I brought her a rose one time. To rehearsal. But I forgot a vase and it di-died."

"That was sweet of you, Roland. Someday you're going to meet a nice girl who appreciates that in a guy. Say, did you go to the dunes that night? The night Lisa drowned?"

170

His eyes shot up at me with what looked like pain. "I wa-wa-wasn't invited," he said, clearly mortified.

"You never went out to the dunes then? To any of the parties?"

He shook his head, looking back down at his feet. I got the feeling he wasn't telling the truth.

"Did you ever go out there, just to watch? Maybe park near the other cars, you know, just to see what was happening?" The way his eyes shot back up I knew I'd hit a nerve.

"Wh-wh-why do you think that?"

"I just wondered, that's all. There's nothing wrong with it." I felt lousy for what I was doing, but I couldn't help myself.

"I wasn't the only one," he blurted, biting his lip. "Others sometimes sa-sat in their cars too. The dunes are pre-pretty at night."

"You have a car?" I asked. "What kind?"

"Dodge m-mini-van. My muh-muh-mother bought it for me so I could come home to visit. She lives up in Lincoln City."

I was trying hard not to let my imagination run away with me, but my palms had gone sweaty and I could feel my heart thumping excitedly. The last victim had been from Lincoln City. And there'd been a rose petal in her palm. And Martha said the killer probably drove a truck or van. And Roland had just admitted that he sometimes went out into the dunes to watch the others.

"Do you want me to es-escort you ho-home?" he asked, gracing me with a crooked smile. "In case Brad and Markie are there?"

"Oh, that's sweet of you, Roland. But right now I'm not going home. You don't like them very much, do you? Markie and Brad?"

"They make fu-fun of me. Because I stutter sometimes. But that's okay. My muh-muh-mother always says that what goes around, comes around." He smiled and in spite of myself, I shivered. "Well, I better let you go," he said, still fidgeting with his shirttail.

Could anyone really be this painfully shy? I wondered. Or was Roland Pipps a better actor than we knew?

"You be careful, okay? My mother says ba-bad things can happen, even if you know they're coming."

"Your mother sounds like a smart lady," I offered.

He looked up quickly through narrowed eyes to see if I was making fun of him. I smiled reassuringly and said good-bye.

As I walked away, I barely resisted the urge to run. Without looking back, I felt Roland watching me all the way down the street.

Chapter Twenty-three

He closed his eyes, feeling the power surge through him, the way it always did before a new adventure. That's how he thought of them now. His little adventures. And though he knew it was reckless and dangerous, he couldn't help himself. He was ready to embark on a new adventure and this time, the victim had come to him.

Chapter Twenty-four

When I got to the corner, I allowed myself a quick peek back and was relieved to see he'd gone. But where had he gone? It was almost dark out and I turned the corner, anxious to put distance between us. Could Roland possibly be the killer? If he'd seen Brad and Markie perform their condom trick, he might have gotten the idea to take the condoms as a way of framing them for his crimes. What was it his mother had said? What goes around comes around? Maybe murdering women was Roland's way of getting even with all the people who made him feel inferior. But it was damned difficult to picture —

chubby, cherubic Roland Pipps performing such hideous, brutal acts.

I'd been walking fast, trying to sort my thoughts, wishing there were someone I could talk to about Roland. When I reached the Performing Arts building, I could hear music from inside. My heart skipped a beat, thinking Lauren might have returned after our set-to. And suddenly, I understood why I'd come this direction. I wanted another chance to explain. In fact, if she wasn't here, I'd just go back to her place. I was tired of running away from my own feelings. It was time to take charge of my emotions.

I pushed the heavy double doors open and peeked inside. The room was dark. Silently, I slipped into the room and stood against a back wall, letting my eyes adjust to the darkness. Classical music blared from somewhere offstage, but there were no other sounds. I tiptoed forward, half-expecting to find Lauren working on props. Suddenly a movement caught my eye and I whirled around toward the orchestra pit.

Mr. Purvis was standing in front of the empty chairs, baton in hand, directing a phantom orchestra to the ominous tones of Beethoven's Fifth. Transfixed, I watched his intense, choppy motions as he batted and punctuated the air. A man possessed, he was totally caught up in the music, lost in another world. I started to back up and bumped into a chair.

Purvis wheeled around, and even in the dim light I could see the sweat that poured off his forehead. His face was flushed. He reminded me of a wild dog I'd surprised once. It had been foraging in the burn barrel behind my house, and we'd seen each other at the same time. We'd stared each other down, both afraid to make a move. Finally, the scroungy predator had slunk off, leaving me breathless, and I realized that he was more afraid of me than I was of him. Purvis had the same frightened, wild look in his eyes now. He was probably embarrassed to have someone barge in on his private performance.

He set his baton down, leaned over and turned off the tape deck at his feet. Suddenly, the room was not only dark, but eerily silent.

"I didn't know I had an audience," he said. His voice sounded strained, as if he didn't know whether to be embarrassed or angry.

"I'm sorry, Mr. Purvis. I didn't know you were here. I came back to finish some work on props for Dr. Monroe."

"I see." He took out a white handkerchief and mopped his brow. He moved into the recesses of the orchestra pit and suddenly the houselights came on. We both blinked at the harshness.

In the light, he seemed much more composed than a moment earlier. His glasses were slightly fogged over, which made his eyes hard to read, but he managed a thin smile.

"I'm afraid you caught me," he said. "Beethoven's my true passion. My real weakness."

"No need to apologize. We all have our weaknesses." I walked toward the stage and leaned against a chair.

"Yes, I suppose we do. Although I understand you were quite the little aggressor today with our Mr. Lewis. Obviously your weaknesses aren't physical ones."

"I think Markie was a little too full of himself, that's all," I said. "Sometimes people need to be brought down a notch or two."

"Oh, but don't they?" he agreed. He walked over to the stage in the funny way he had of moving and perched on the edge, letting his legs swing free. "Working at this level, you have to put up with things you'd never do otherwise. I have to keep reminding myself that they are only boys, but still, the urge to throttle them sometimes is nearly overwhelming. I'd have enjoyed seeing you — let's see, how did Rita put it? — kick Markie's scrawny little ass halfway across the dunes?" His lips curled into a tight smile.

"Well, it's not something I'm particularly proud of," I

said, realizing this wasn't entirely true. I'd enjoyed kicking Markie's ass. He deserved it. "Speaking of working with boys," I added, hoping the segue would work, "what do you think of Roland Pipps?"

"What do I think of him in what way?" His small eyes regarded me with caution.

"Well, I was wondering about his stuttering, for one thing. Someone said he never stuttered onstage until today. Why do you think that is?"

"Roland is a very special boy," Purvis said. "He has a rare talent buried beneath a great deal of baggage. He was abused, I'm quite sure of it. And children can be terribly ruthless to someone different. The slightest handicap can result in complete ostracism." He patted his springy red hair and looked up at the ceiling.

"There is no limit to the cruelties that young people can heap on one another. I believe Roland's stuttering today onstage may be something serious indeed. I think he's ready for some kind of breakthrough. On the other hand, he could be nearing a breakdown. The pressure a boy like Roland puts on himself just to get through an ordinary day can be overwhelming. I see Roland on the verge of emerging, but into what, who can say?"

"You seem to know a lot about him," I offered.

"Oh, not really. I studied psychology in college, along with music, of course. And I recognize so many of Roland's symptoms. You see, not long ago, I wasn't all that different from Roland myself." He looked straight at me, challenging me to find fault with this admission.

"You stuttered?" I asked, hoping my voice had remained neutral.

He let out a bark of a laugh. "No. My handicap was far worse. I was ugly." He pulled up the sleeve of his jacket and revealed a withered arm so scarred from burns the skin resembled rubber. "Would you like to see my legs?" he asked, finally allowing himself a full smile. "Or my neck?" He tugged his shirt collar down to reveal more mottled rubber. "Just a little childhood accident. My mother was a careless woman."

It took me a moment to digest this. "No wonder you're so sensitive to Roland," I finally said, hoping I sounded empathetic and not just full of pity.

"Yes, well. Like I said, I believe Roland will come out on top in the end. But it is painful to watch the process of transition. Change is very often tortuous."

"Do you think Roland is capable of violence?" I blurted. I was amazed at this psychological profile he was painting. If he was right, Roland was sounding more and more like someone capable of the grisly crimes I'd begun to suspect him of.

"If not yet, I dare say it won't be long now." He seemed almost wistful. "But then, who isn't? You yourself exhibited a tidy bit of violence this afternoon. By the way, did you ever find the photos Markie seemed so upset over?"

I hesitated, not sure how much to say.

"So you did," he said, smiling his tight-lipped smile again.

"Why do you say that?"

"People who've been through things like I have develop a rather keen sense of perception. As a child, of course, I was aware of the slightest nuances. I knew when people were repulsed. Which was often. You learn to detect falsehood easily. And you, my dear, are not a very proficient liar."

"I wasn't aware I had lied." I was beginning to feel uneasy.

"Oh, but you were about to. Tell me, did you find the pictures interesting? Tantalizing? Revealing?"

"No. The sight of Markie's naked body didn't do much for me, if that's what you mean."

"No, I don't suppose it would. Still, there are plenty of

178

girls who seem to find him attractive. But you're not that kind of girl at all, are you?"

I wasn't sure where this was going. Was he referring to my lesbianism? Or was he flirting with me? Either way, I was growing increasingly uneasy.

"I'm not sure how to answer that," I said truthfully. "Listen, Mr. Purvis. I appreciate your insights into Roland, but I've got to be going now." I started for the double doors and to my dismay he hopped off the stage and followed after me.

"What? Not going to work on the props like you'd intended? I hope I didn't do or say anything to upset you." He touched me lightly on the elbow and I involuntarily jerked away. When I looked up, his face looked as though I'd slapped him. I felt instant guilt.

"No, it's not that," I said. "It's just that I've remembered something I need to do. I hadn't realized how late it was getting." Which was true. Outside, darkness had set in.

"Well, let me give you a lift," he said, holding the door open for me. "My car's right over here."

He headed across the parking lot toward a small, red Honda Civic. I had no desire to get in his car, even though my legs were tired. My second trek through the dunes had taken its toll and my calf muscles ached with each step. He opened the trunk of the Civic and retrieved his briefcase from inside. I'd stopped walking, frozen in indecision.

"Well, come on," he insisted. "I may be ugly, but it's not contagious. Where can I drop you?"

Oh, what the hell, I thought. I'd let him drop me down the street from Rhonda's. "Elm Street," I said.

"Okey-dokey." He beamed. "Here, let's take this one. My Honda's low on gas." He took me by the elbow again and I dared not insult him by cringing, though his touch repulsed me for reasons I couldn't identify. Before I knew

179

what was happening, he'd stepped past the Honda toward a brown van parked nose to nose with it. I stopped in my tracks, suddenly petrified. Then I turned and ran.

Before I'd taken three steps, Purvis sprang forward and slammed his briefcase into the back of my head, knocking me sideways. I tried to right myself, but he yanked me back toward the passenger door of the van, his bony fingers digging into my arm. With a quickness and strength that belied his size, and despite my frantic efforts to pull free, he managed to shove me into the van and slam the door behind me.

As soon as he stepped away from the door, I reached for the handle but there was none. I pounded the door, then lunged across the front seat toward the driver's side. Before I could reach the handle, Purvis was already sliding in beside me. He turned to me and offered a terrifying smile, shattering any doubts I had about who the killer was.

"What's your hurry, girl? I thought you wanted a ride." He started the engine and backed carefully out of the lot. My mind raced, searching for an escape. If I was right about the killer choosing strong, defiant women, maybe my only chance was to try submission. I considered this tactic, risking a quick glance to the back of the van, noticing all at once the sickeningly sweet odor that permeated the interior, and the sheet of plywood he'd placed behind the front seat, blocking off the rear of the van.

"I want you to pull over and let me out," I said. So much for strategy, I thought. I pushed repeatedly on the window lever, but it was locked.

Purvis threw back his head and laughed. "Oh, you do, do you? Well, let's see. Elm Street. That's where Lisa Lane used to live, isn't it?"

"I wouldn't know," I said.

"Uh, uh, uh. You're lying again. Remember, I told you I'm very sensitive about these things." He shook his forefinger in the air as if at a naughty child. "I'll just drop you right at her house if you like. Or down the street a ways, if you prefer."

"Wherever. That'll be fine."

"Yes. Yes, it will." His voice had taken on a singsong quality that scared me more than anything he'd said or done so far.

"I believe it's just down from here." He pulled the van to the curb and killed the engine. "Is this all right?"

What kind of sick game was he playing, now? I stared at him coldly, knowing there was no way out of the van.

"Here, let me assist you." He hopped down from his seat and came around to the passenger's side, using his key to open my door. His glasses were fogged up again, but behind the haze I could see the craziness in his eyes.

When he opened the door, I kicked out with both feet, catching him in the midsection. He stumbled backwards, but not far enough. He tried to slam the door, but I managed to wedge my body between the door and van. The door caught my knee and my leg buckled.

"You shouldn't have done that," he said, clucking his tongue. He grabbed my hair in his fist and yanked me down from the van. Before I could make a move, he had twisted my arm behind my back and was pushing me down the street toward Rhonda's townhouse.

Surely someone would see us, I prayed. But the street was quiet and dark. My arm felt close to breaking and tears sprang up in my eyes, as much from fear as from pain. But Purvis was whistling softly, his lips just inches from my face. Even if someone had passed by, we probably looked like lovers, taking an evening stroll. When we got to Rhonda's, he marched me up the steps to the door.

"Go ahead and knock," he whispered. "When she asks who it is, just say Cassidy. Otherwise, I'll have to break this arm. Okay?"

I nodded, fighting against the pain and fear. With any luck, Rhonda would be gone. Maybe Martha had already come and gone. I knocked softly, praying for no answer.

"Who is it?" Rhonda's voice rang out. Purvis tightened his grip on my arm and I nearly buckled.

"Rhonda, it's a trap!"

"Cassidy, is that you?"

The door flew open and before Rhonda could see what was happening, before I could make a move, Purvis had pushed us both inside, grabbed Rhonda by the throat and slammed the door.

Chapter Twenty-five

The second batch of photos was spread out on the coffee table and as soon as my gaze went to them, Purvis saw them. He'd let go of my arm and I was rubbing it gently, trying to restore the circulation. It wasn't broken, but it felt as if my shoulder had been pulled out of its socket.

He took his hand away from Rhonda's mouth and whispered into her ear. "You make a single sound and you're a dead woman."

She nodded and he pushed both of us toward the couch. Even if my arm had been a hundred percent, his threat to Rhonda was enough to keep me from trying anything rash.

"Well, well, well. Little Lisa did herself proud. Although as I suspected, these really don't show any details. Still, it wouldn't do to have them lying around. Where are the negatives?"

Rhonda's gaze darted to me and I gave her one brief shake of the head. Purvis caught the exchange.

"You're not thinking of wasting my time?" he asked, looking at me with eyes that had grown as cold and flat as wet stones.

"The police already have the negatives," I said.

"Tsk, tsk," he said, shaking his head. "You're a much slower learner than I thought. But not to worry. I have no intention of trashing the place again. And Rhonda's not going to get the negatives either. You are. Because if you don't, I'm going to slice her up right in front of you." His right hand slipped down the front of his trousers and he pulled out a long thin switchblade. With a flick, the six-inch blade shot out from the handle and before Rhonda could even dodge, Purvis had his hand to her throat.

Rhonda's eyes bulged, but she didn't utter a sound. Purvis drew the blade tenderly across her throat and a tiny line of red bubbled to the surface.

"Get them," he said.

Without another hesitation, I went to retrieve the negatives from the back of Rhonda's teddy bear. The first set of prints were still in my pocket. I considered hiding them somewhere, but if Purvis managed to kill us both, I wanted Martha to be able to find the prints. They were probably better off in my pocket.

"Good girl," he said when I handed him the negatives. He held them up to the light and examined them, making sure I hadn't left out the two incriminating shots.

"Your arm still hurt?" he asked, sounding for all the world like he really cared. He'd eased his hold on Rhonda, resting his knife hand on her shoulder. They looked like sweethearts sitting on the sofa watching TV. Except for the trickle of blood on her throat, I thought.

"I think it's broken," I said.

"Oh, no. You'd know if it were. Here. Inside my brief-case, you'll find some nylon rope. Get it for me, would you?" His voice was casually polite, as if I were helping him make tea. But his eyes continued to dart around the room, like a man hyped on speed. And he kept licking his lips, as if the excitement of the moment were too much for him.

I dug in the leather case and pulled out a neatly coiled length of rope. I held it out to him, wondering when and how I'd be able to make a move. With my left arm nearly immobilized, I was at a distinct disadvantage. Not to mention the switchblade.

"Oh, no. You do the honors. I'm sure you can manage to tie up your friend. Your arm's not broken, after all. I'll be here to supervise."

Reluctantly, I stood in front of Rhonda and wound the rope around her ankles.

"Tighter," he commanded.

"There's no point in cutting off her circulation."

"There's no point in dropping a baby in scalding water for spilling milk, either. Is there?"

I looked up, my mind scrambling. "Is that what happened? Your mother abused you? That's terrible." If nothing else, talking about himself might take his mind off my tying Rhonda. If possible, I wanted to leave her some wriggle room. Suddenly, Purvis leaped to his feet and I held my breath. He moved close behind me and reached around, his hot breath tickling my neck. With his right hand, he sliced the knife through the nylon rope, cutting it in two.

"Now do her hands," he directed. "And you know absolutely nothing about my mother. Nothing about how horrible what she did was. So don't, for God's sake, try using any psychobabble on me. I'm the one who studied

185

psychology, after all. You don't think I understand my own perversities? Things happen for a reason. Had I not endured a lifetime of suffering and humiliation, I might not have evolved into what I am today. Though I don't suppose you look at that the same way I do."

"How else is there to look at it? You murder people. No matter how horrible your childhood, nothing gives you the right to take someone else's life." My heart was thundering. It probably wasn't the smartest tactic to tick this guy off. But if I could divert his attention from what I was doing, I had a better chance of succeeding. I moved Rhonda's hands apart so that it would appear I was tying them tightly, but leaving some space between her skin and the ropes. It was tricky with my left arm so useless.

His sudden bark of laughter made me start, raising goose bumps on my arms.

"I don't need someone to give me the right," he said. "I take it. People like you, who've been given rights and privileges your whole life, are totally blind to those who, for one reason or another, are denied those same rights. I got tired of being denied. And one day, I realized I didn't need anyone else's permission. That was the day I was reborn, so to speak. The day I became all-powerful."

Not only did Purvis think he could justify his grotesque perversion, he thought he was omnipotent. I could no longer conceal the trembling in my voice. "What rights were you denied?" I asked.

Again, his laughter chilled me. "How about the right to pursue happiness? How about the right to ask a girl on a date and have her accept? Just once. To kiss a girl who doesn't cringe. To touch someone and not make them shudder with revulsion. Is that too much to ask?" He was waving the knife as he spoke, thrusting it in the air with each point.

"You've never dated?"

He patted the orange frizz from his forehead, heedless of the metal blade in his hand. "When in school, even college, I did try. I didn't want to go everywhere alone, forever the outcast. I had a few friends who invited me to tag along, but it was always so achingly obvious. I was the proverbial fifth wheel. The ugly duck, the pathetic loser. Girls loathed me. The harder I tried to impress them, the more they'd look at me with revulsion. Disdain! But a funny thing happened. After a while, the idea of making them cringe and shudder started to have a different effect on me. That's when I realized they no longer had any power over me. It was I who had the power." His pale eyes gleamed with craziness, and a ghastly smile spread across his thin lips. I could feel Rhonda tremble beside me.

Suddenly, there was an urgent knocking at the door. All three of us froze, and my racing pulse slammed into overdrive. Could it be Martha? Purvis held his fingers to his lips and moved in behind Rhonda, resting the knife blade against her throat again.

"Rhonda? Open up. It's Gracie. Cassidy's friend. Lauren thinks she knows whose van that is. She needs to see the pictures! Come on, Rhonda. Open the door!"

"Well, well, well," Purvis said quietly. "Good thing we parked down the street." He put his finger to his lips again, urging Rhonda to remain silent, then brought his knife to my throat and walked me to the door. He pulled it open without saying a word.

Gracie's smile ended midstream. Lauren blanched.

"Step inside, ladies. Unless you want me to decapitate her right here."

Lauren and Gracie slowly inched past us into the room. In one swift motion, Purvis locked the door behind them.

"Well, Dr. Monroe. Imagine meeting you here, like this." Purvis's voice had gone back to the singsong quality that scared me the most.

"Philip. What's going on?" she asked. But the terror in her eyes told me she already knew.

"Well, it looks like this is my lucky day," he said. "I was in the mood for a date. It looks like I'll have my hands full tonight. A veritable orgy. You," he said, pointing a long index finger at Gracie. "Take that rope there and tie these two together. Make it snappy."

Gracie bunched her hands into fists, but there was little she could do but comply. She retrieved the rope and told Lauren and me to stand back to back.

"Not that way. Have them turn to face each other. Tie them wrist to wrist, ankle to ankle. Wrap it around their bodies. That's it. Tighter."

"Phil, we can get you help," Lauren said.

He threw his head back and laughed. "Tell her, Cassidy. Do I look like the kind of man who wants help?"

"Yes," I said. "I think you do."

"Liar!" he shouted, startling us all. For the first time, I caught a glimpse of his rage. "I do not want help! I don't need help! I am quite satisfied with my life. Right now I am ecstatic! The four of you will be my grand farewell to the Oregon Coast. Then it's off to greener pastures." He was shouting like a madman. But then, that's exactly what he was.

"You won't get away with this," I said.

"Oh, yes I will." The anger in his voice disappeared as quickly as it had arisen. He was back to singsong. "In just a jiffy, I'm going to back my van right up to this door and help you ladies into it. I found a deserted field the other day that should be just perfect. We'll have to cancel the play, of course. Everyone will be so distraught over Dr. Monroe's death." He emitted a high-pitched giggle.

Gracie had managed to tie Lauren and me together from ankle to shoulder while leaving a cushion of air between us. Purvis strode over toward us and took the rest of the rope from Gracie's hands. The knife was still clutched in his right hand and he held it to Gracie's face.

"Kneel down," he commanded, slicing off another section of rope. Gracie started to do so, but then, with lightening speed, she brought her knee upward, connecting with Purvis's crotch. The blade shot forward and blood spurted out of Gracie's shoulder. Within seconds, he was on top of her, snarling like a wild beast. Gracie covered her head with her hands to ward off the blows while he furiously wound the rope around her like a rodeo cowboy tying up a calf. It was all over before it started. Even Gracie was no match for the crazed beast that Purvis had become.

Without saying another word, he left to get his van.

"Did Martha call?" I asked Rhonda.

"I haven't heard from anyone," she said, trying not to cry.

"I'm sorry," Gracie said. "I thought I could take him."

"Are you all right?" Lauren asked. She looked more shaken than any of us. Her face was ashen and I could feel her body tremble against mine.

Gracie nodded, but the blood seeping from the gash in her left arm spoke for itself.

"What are we going to do now?" Lauren asked, her eyes searching mine. We were so close together, I couldn't see them clearly — just the intensity of the blue.

"We start working to get our hands free. Rhonda, I tried to tie yours loosely. See if you can bring your hands together and slip out of the rope."

"What do you think I have been doing?" she said, sounding close to tears.

"How about you, Gracie?"

"He's got me wrapped up pretty good. I don't stand a chance. I did try to leave you guys some room to work. See if you can work your hands free."

Lauren's right hand was tied to my left, her left to my right as we faced each other. We were connected at the wrists, but Gracie had left the loops fairly loose. Still, neither of us could get our hands to slip through.

"Quit fighting me," Lauren whispered. "We've got to work together."

I bit my tongue. This was no time to bring up the fact that she'd been fighting me ever since we'd met. We were

189

still no closer to freedom when the sound of the van's engine revved at the front door.

"If anyone manages to get a hand free, make a little cough so the rest of us will know. There're four of us. Somehow, we've got to be able to overcome him."

"He's strong, Cass," Gracie said. It was true. With the sudden burst of rage I'd just seen him use on Gracie, I knew we'd have trouble taking him on, even if all four of us were untied. But we needed to be ready.

Purvis bounded back through the door, looking exuberant. He had a soaked handkerchief in his hand and the sickening sweet smell of chloroform stung my nose as soon as he entered. He walked to where Rhonda was still seated on the sofa and held the cloth to her mouth. She fought back for only a few seconds and then her head lolled to one side. He stuffed a different rag into her mouth, so that when she woke, she wouldn't be able to scream. He then hefted her over his shoulder and with an ease that surprised me, toted her through the door and into the back of the van. The rest of us watched with utter dread.

"You next, Tarzan," he said to Gracie when he reappeared. He was, I was pleased to note, a little winded. I saw the muscles bunch in Gracie's jaw, but there was little she could do. Once she was out, he stuffed a handkerchief into her slack mouth and dragged her across the floor to the front door. Rhonda wasn't any lightweight, but Gracie was more than he could handle.

I felt Lauren's body tense against mine, but I could think of nothing to say or do that would calm her. I was as scared as she was. We heard the back of the van door close and the sound of another vehicle pull up. I strained to listen, but my heart was pounding so loudly I couldn't hear anything else.

"Help me get to the window!" I said. Together we

hopped sideways and with great effort managed to move the curtain aside so that we could peek out.

"Martha!" I yelled. But she was already moving back to her Bronco, waving a thanks toward Purvis who was smiling and waving back. Lauren and I jumped up and down, yelling, but it was no use. Martha drove off without ever looking back.

"That was close," Purvis said, coming back in. "I almost had to take me a fifth lady. I'm not sure the van is big enough." I was relieved to see he hadn't brought any more chloroform rags with him.

"You two will have to help me out, okay? Time is suddenly of the essence." Back to his polite, tea-and-crumpets voice. "Just hop on over to the door and I'll help you in. It's time we get moving." He patted Lauren on the rear and I felt her cringe. As an added incentive, he waved the switchblade beneath her nose. Her already pale face went absolutely white. "Hop to," he said.

We did. He opened the front door, peered in both directions and then walked the few steps to the van, opening the rear. He motioned us forward and when we stopped in front of the van, he shoved us onto the hard floor. He pushed at our feet until we'd been shoved all the way in and then threw Lauren's purse in after us before slamming the door.

The chloroform smell was nauseating, but there was another stench in the van that was far worse. He'd tried to cover it with some flowery freshener, but the smell of death still permeated the interior, making it nearly impossible to breathe.

"I'm scared," Lauren whispered. We were on our sides, inches from each other, our bodies touching along our entire lengths.

"So am I," I said. I closed my eyes and let my cheek rest against Lauren's. A single, salty tear seeped down her cheek and before I knew what I was doing, I brushed it away with my lips.

"Your timing's a little off," she said. But she did smile.

"Don't I know it," I answered. I laid my cheek against hers again and tried to comfort her the only way I could.

Both Gracie and Rhonda were starting to stir, but they were nowhere near coherent. The driver's door finally clanged shut and the van began moving. The back of the van was windowless, and with the partition separating us from the front, I had no way of looking out. I tried to visualize which way we were going.

"Let's keep trying with our hands," I whispered. I knew Purvis could hear us if we spoke any louder. I could hear him whistling in the front seat. We struggled with the ropes until we were both exhausted and gave up again.

"My arm is killing me," Lauren said. So was mine, for that matter. We'd both been lying on our sides, and the trapped arms beneath our bodies had gone numb.

"Let's roll over," I whispered. We rocked twice and managed to tumble over. Now I was lying directly on top of her. The relief for my arm was immediate and intense. I tried to ignore all other sensations and concentrate on getting free.

The van continued to bump and wind its way what I sensed was eastward while I tried to think of something to do. I couldn't see my watch, but I felt like we'd been on the road at least fifteen minutes when the van suddenly slowed and gravel crunched beneath the tires. He had taken a side road and I feared it wouldn't be long before he reached his destination.

"I'd give anything to have my Swiss Army knife," I said. It was sitting on my dresser at home.

"I have one in my purse," Lauren said.

I stared at her in disbelief. We had wasted nearly twenty minutes! Without another word, we inched our bodies over to where the purse had fallen. Some of its contents had spilled out, but unfortunately the knife was not among them.

"In the little zippered pouch," she whispered. It was almost impossible to coordinate our movements because there was so little wiggle room. I tried to make my arm relax while Lauren's fingers dug for the knife. I was beginning to think she'd never find it when she let out a hushed cry of triumph. "I don't know if we can get it open," she said. She held the small red handle while I pried at the metal edges. My nails kept slipping and I gouged Lauren's hand a few times, but she remained stoic. I almost sobbed with relief when I finally managed to pull one of the blades out. Unfortunately, I'd opened the nail file.

Trying not to panic, I went to work again and this time opened the small knife blade with relative ease. "I've got it!" I whispered.

Even in the dark interior, I could see the relief in her eyes.

The knife was new and the little blade was sharp. Even so, it took several minutes to work it through the nylon rope that bound our wrists. I had to saw upward at a very difficult angle, and both our hands were bleeding by the time the rope was finally severed.

"Untie our feet," I whispered. While she worked on that end with her free left hand I used my right to cut through the rope around our other wrists. We worked feverishly, trying not to rock the van as it bumped along the gravel road. It was awkward, but for once, we weren't fighting against each other.

By the time we had freed ourselves, the van was starting to climb and had slowed to a mere crawl. I crept over to Gracie and pulled the rag from her mouth, then went to work on her ropes. Lauren did the same for

Rhonda, who had started to moan. Both women peered through the dark with groggy, terror-filled eyes as we untied them.

I held my finger to my lips and they both nodded, but I could tell their minds had not cleared from the chloroform. The sudden fresh air was helping though, and both of them gulped it into their lungs.

Suddenly the van lurched to a halt. The four of us froze. I glanced at the back door, but it was too late to make a run for it. I could already hear Purvis whistling his way back toward the rear door.

"What are we going to do?" Lauren whispered. There was no time to answer. Even if I'd had an answer, which I didn't.

The door creaked open and I could just make out Purvis's smile in the dark. "Ladies, did you enjoy the ride?"

Before he could take in the situation, I dove for his midsection, giving it all I had.

Purvis fell backward and landed hard on the ground with me on top of him. But before I could even raise the little Army knife, I heard the familiar snick of his switch-blade and just had time to roll to my left before the thin blade could slice through me.

He turned to face me, his lips snarling like a wild beast's. His eyes were flat with hatred. I stood and waved the red Swiss Army knife at him, challenging him to come after me. He did.

As soon as he turned toward me, Lauren leaped out of the van and charged his back. He stumbled forward, nearly falling again just a foot from where I stood. He turned and glared at her savagely while I backed up.

"You might as well forget it, Purvis. There are four of us. Just put the knife down." My voice did not sound as convincing as I'd have liked. Purvis looked from Lauren to me, unable to decide who to attack first.

He finally took a step toward me and when he did,

Gracie staggered out of the van, her belt doubled over in her fist. Before he could reach me, Gracie snapped the belt forward with a flick of the wrist and the metal buckle caught Purvis just behind the ear. He whirled around and charged her like an enraged bull.

She flicked the belt again and caught him full in the face. His glasses flew off and his nose erupted in blood.

He stopped in his tracks, clutching at his nose. I moved in behind him and saw Rhonda step out of the van with Lauren's purse. She was whirling it around her head like a lasso.

At the same time, Lauren walked over and stepped on Purvis's glasses. The sound of crunching glass made him go berserk.

He charged Lauren and as he did, I dove for his ankles, hoping I could knock him off balance before he reached her. Gracie apparently had the same idea. As I tripped him in midair, Gracie's leg shot out Karate-style and caught him squarely on the chin. His head snapped back and he tumbled to the ground in a heap. His flat eyes rolled upward and, after a few moments of fluttering, rolled shut.

"Get the rope," I said. The switchblade was still clutched in his hand but Purvis had been knocked unconscious. Even so, I held my knife in position as I carefully pried the switchblade from his fingers, careful not to smear his prints.

Gracie was clutching the shoulder that Purvis had sliced back at the house.

"Let's look at that," I said.

She removed her hand and when I saw the extent of the damage, I felt queasy. The wound was deep and bleeding freely after the sudden activity. I took off my jacket and wrapped it around her arm while Lauren and Rhonda began tying Purvis.

"You really thought you could take him with that puny knife?" she asked, grimacing.

"I was counting on you the whole way, Tarzan," I answered. Despite her obvious pain, she grinned.

A noise, which had started in the distance, grew louder and we looked up through the night sky at the noisy descent of an approaching helicopter. Dirt flew up around us as the chopper touched down, its bright spotlight temporarily blinding us. Before it had even finished landing, Martha Harper leaped out with the two rookie FBI agents right behind her, their guns extended. When she saw Purvis's trussed-up body, Martha holstered her revolver and jogged toward us. She wrapped me up in a big bear hug and swung me around in a circle, nearly crushing my ribs. Finally, she put me down and stepped back to look at the others, shaking her head. The FBI agents stood over Purvis, who had begun to moan unintelligibly.

"Damn! One of you girls musta been a Girl Scout!" the shorter FBI agent said, shining his flashlight at the elaborate manner in which Purvis had been bound. I had to admit, he did rather resemble a mummy. Rhonda was beaming from ear to ear.

"You done good, kiddo," Martha said. "I swear to God, I thought we'd lost you. When I saw him in the driveway, I knew I needed to call for backup. Shit, this one was too close." There were tears in her usually steady eyes. "Without the chopper, we might not've caught up with you. Are you okay?"

"Gracie's got a pretty deep cut," I said. All three of them looked at the blood seeping from Gracie's shoulder and blanched.

"We need to get her to a hospital," Martha said.

"The crime scene division and crime lab techs are on the way," the taller agent said to Martha. "If you want, we can take her back in the chopper with this piece of shit while you take the others' statements." He nudged Purvis sharply with the toe of his black boot, eliciting another pathetic moan. "Or Pierce can take the statements if you want to ride back with me." His tone was just condescending enough to make Martha bristle.

"I think we'd rather give our statements to Detective Harper," I said. "After all, she's the one who figured out the college connection. If it weren't for her, you all would probably still be looking in flower shops up in Lincoln City."

Martha shot me a black look but I couldn't help myself. I smiled sweetly at the agents who glowered back.

"Yeah, well, just don't touch anything in the van," the taller one hissed. I felt Martha tense beside me as the agents dragged Purvis to his feet and started to push him toward the helicopter. Suddenly, the taller one stopped and looked back at Martha. "Oh, and another thing." He paused, then went on with a stern look. "Your gal pal here is absolutely right. It looks like we owe you an apology, Detective Harper." He managed a grin. "And I'll make sure that bozo you work for knows the score." He and Martha locked eyes until finally, Martha acknowledged the compliment with a small nod of her own.

It wasn't much, but as we watched them carry Purvis to the helicopter with Gracie tagging along behind them, I sensed the tension that had been building in Martha for so long finally begin to dissipate.

"So," she said after the roar of the chopper diminished. "Let me guess." She took a step toward Lauren, grinning widely. "You wouldn't by any chance be the drama professor?"

Chapter Twenty-six

As the chopper lifted off, he came to and peered out at the group of women below. They were his type, all right. Any one of them would have been just fine. He could picture sinking his teeth into their flesh, tearing off any part he wanted.

It was all that stupid Lisa Lane's fault, he thought. Dumb bitch didn't know what she was doing. He'd been so careful, too. Hadn't even given into the urge, the terrible longing he had, to gnaw on her. It had taken more control than he'd ever mustered, just to drag her into the water and hold her under until she quit kicking.

He'd chased her first, of course. When she saw him, she

dropped that stupid camera and ran. Luckily, she was dumb enough to run toward the water. He hadn't had to drag her far. But when he went back for the camera, he couldn't find it. Exhausted, more from the restraint he'd shown than the effort of killing the bitch, he gave up. That was the only mistake he'd made.

He closed his eyes as the group of women below grew smaller and smaller. He didn't really need them, he thought. As long as he had his memories, he'd be all right. And someday, he'd get out. Then, he wouldn't need his memories at all. He'd make new ones.

Chapter Twenty-seven

The houselights were dimmed and the stage lights were burning fiercely. After much deliberation, the cast had decided that despite all, the show would go on. The assistant conductor insisted he could lead the orchestra, and though Lauren had been hoping against hope that they'd vote otherwise, here they were on opening night, and the house was packed.

Of course, all the publicity over Purvis being the serial killer hadn't hurt the attendance one bit.

Lauren and I were sitting in the last row in what she maintained were the best seats in the house. As the lights came up, I reached over and squeezed her hand. Suddenly

Markie Lewis strode onto stage, his booming voice reverberating throughout the theater. The makeup under his eye didn't quite hide his shiner.

"I still can't believe Roland Pipps decked him," I whispered.

"He was protecting your honor!" Lauren whispered back, grinning. "I think Roland's quite smitten with you."

Martha had told us that when she'd gone looking for me at the little apartment I'd been using, she'd found three boys engaged in a knock-down, drag-out fight. She'd managed to break it up, but not before Roland Pipps succeeded in giving both Markie and Brad Capers black eyes. He'd done it with his bare fists, she said. But I knew it wasn't just his fists. It was the sheer rage that had built up after years of abuse. Thank God Roland had taken it out on the ones who deserved it, I thought. The idea of him turning into another Purvis made me shudder.

Brad sauntered onto the stage looking quite lordly, despite his own shiner, and played a surprisingly realistic Jesus. But the show was absolutely stolen by Roland Pipps.

Purvis had been right about one thing. Roland had been ripe for a transition, and nowhere was it more apparent than onstage that night. As the imperious Pontius Pilate, he reigned. He strutted and preened and sang his heart out. There was not a stammer or stutter to be heard. When the play was over, it was Roland who brought on the standing ovation.

"You did it," I said, whispering into Lauren's ear so she could hear me over the applause.

She smiled at me, her blue eyes dancing.

"Yes, well, I don't know about you," she said, whispering back, "but I thought Mary Jane's dress was a little long. You up for another hemming job this evening?"

"Only if I get to do the pinning," I said.

She leaned so close, her lips almost brushed my ear. "You're on."

LOOKING FOR NAIAD?

Buy our books at
www.naiadpress.com

or call our toll-free number
1-800-533-1973

or by fax (24 hours a day)
1-850-539-9731

A few of the publications of
THE NAIAD PRESS, INC.
P.O. Box 10543   Tallahassee, Florida 32302
Phone (850) 539-5965
Toll-Free Order Number: 1-800-533-1973
Web Site: WWW.NAIADPRESS.COM
Mail orders welcome. Please include 15% postage.
Write or call for our free catalog which also features an
incredible selection of lesbian videos.

FIFTH WHEEL by Kate Calloway. 224 pp. 5th Cassidy James
mystery.   ISBN 1-56280-218-6 $11.95

JUST YESTERDAY by Linda Hill. 176 pp. Reliving all the
passion of yesterday.   ISBN 1-56280-219-4   11.95

THE TOUCH OF YOUR HAND edited by Barbara Grier and
Christine Cassidy. 304 pp. Erotic love stories by Naiad Press
authors.   ISBN 1-56280-220-8   14.95

WINDROW GARDEN by Janet McClellan. 192 pp. They discover
a passion they never dreamed possible.   ISBN 1-56280-216-X   11.95

PAST DUE by Claire McNab. 224 pp. 10th Carol Ashton
mystery.   ISBN 1-56280-217-8   11.95

CHRISTABEL by Laura Adams. 224 pp. Two captive hearts and
the passion that will set them free.   ISBN 1-56280-214-3   11.95

PRIVATE PASSIONS by Laura DeHart Young. 192 pp. An
unforgettable new portrait of lesbian love . . .   ISBN 1-56280-215-1   11.95

BAD MOON RISING by Barbara Johnson. 208 pp. 2nd Colleen
Fitzgerald mystery.   ISBN 1-56280-211-9   11.95

RIVER QUAY by Janet McClellan. 208 pp. 3rd Tru North
mystery.   ISBN 1-56280-212-7   11.95

ENDLESS LOVE by Lisa Shapiro. 272 pp. To believe, once
again, that love can be forever.   ISBN 1-56280-213-5   11.95

FALLEN FROM GRACE by Pat Welch. 256 pp. 6th Helen Black
mystery.   ISBN 1-56280-209-7   11.95

THE NAKED EYE by Catherine Ennis. 208 pp. Her lover in the
camera's eye . . .   ISBN 1-56280-210-0   11.95

OVER THE LINE by Tracey Richardson. 176 pp. 2nd Stevie
Houston mystery.   ISBN 1-56280-202-X   11.95

JULIA'S SONG by Ann O'Leary. 208 pp. Strangely
disturbing . . . strangely exciting.   ISBN 1-56280-197-X   11.95

LOVE IN THE BALANCE by Marianne K. Martin. 256 pp.
Weighing the costs of love . . .   ISBN 1-56280-199-6   11.95

PIECE OF MY HEART by Julia Watts. 208 pp. All the
stuff that dreams are made of —   ISBN 1-56280-206-2   11.95

MAKING UP FOR LOST TIME by Karin Kallmaker. 240 pp.
Nobody does it better . . .   ISBN 1-56280-196-1   11.95

GOLD FEVER by Lyn Denison. 224 pp. By author of *Dream
Lover.*   ISBN 1-56280-201-1   11.95

WHEN THE DEAD SPEAK by Therese Szymanski. 224 pp. 2nd
Brett Higgins mystery.   ISBN 1-56280-198-8   11.95

FOURTH DOWN by Kate Calloway. 240 pp. 4th Cassidy James
mystery.   ISBN 1-56280-205-4   11.95

A MOMENT'S INDISCRETION by Peggy J. Herring. 176 pp.
There's a fine line between love and lust . . .   ISBN 1-56280-194-5   11.95

CITY LIGHTS/COUNTRY CANDLES by Penny Hayes. 208 pp.
About the women she has known . . .   ISBN 1-56280-195-3   11.95

POSSESSIONS by Kaye Davis. 240 pp. 2nd Maris Middleton
mystery.   ISBN 1-56280-192-9   11.95

A QUESTION OF LOVE by Saxon Bennett. 208 pp. Every
woman is granted one great love.   ISBN 1-56280-205-4   11.95

RHYTHM TIDE by Frankie J. Jones. 160 pp.   . . . to desire
passionately and be passionately desired.   ISBN 1-56280-189-9   11.95

PENN VALLEY PHOENIX by Janet McClellan. 208 pp. 2nd
Tru North Mystery.   ISBN 1-56280-200-3   11.95

BY RESERVATION ONLY by Jackie Calhoun. 240 pp. A
chance for true happiness.   ISBN 1-56280-191-0   11.95

OLD BLACK MAGIC by Jaye Maiman. 272 pp. 9th Robin
Miller mystery.   ISBN 1-56280-175-9   11.95

LEGACY OF LOVE by Marianne K. Martin. 240 pp. Women
will do anything for her . . .   ISBN 1-56280-184-8   11.95

LETTING GO by Ann O'Leary. 160 pp. Laura, at 39, in love
with 23-year-old Kate.   ISBN 1-56280-183-X   11.95

LADY BE GOOD edited by Barbara Grier and Christine Cassidy.
288 pp. Erotic stories by Naiad Press authors.   ISBN 1-56280-180-5   14.95

CHAIN LETTER by Claire McNab. 288 pp. 9th Carol Ashton
mystery.   ISBN 1-56280-181-3   11.95

NIGHT VISION by Laura Adams. 256 pp. Erotic fantasy romance
by "famous" author.   ISBN 1-56280-182-1   11.95

SEA TO SHINING SEA by Lisa Shapiro. 256 pp. Unable to resist
the raging passion . . .   ISBN 1-56280-177-5   11.95

THIRD DEGREE by Kate Calloway. 224 pp. 3rd Cassidy James
mystery.   ISBN 1-56280-185-6   11.95

WHEN THE DANCING STOPS by Therese Szymanski. 272 pp.
1st Brett Higgins mystery. ISBN 1-56280-186-4   11.95

PHASES OF THE MOON by Julia Watts. 192 pp. . . . . hungry
for everything life has to offer. ISBN 1-56280-176-7   11.95

BABY IT'S COLD by Jaye Maiman. 256 pp. 5th Robin Miller
mystery. ISBN 1-56280-156-2   10.95

CLASS REUNION by Linda Hill. 176 pp. The girl from her
past . . . ISBN 1-56280-178-3   11.95

DREAM LOVER by Lyn Denison. 224 pp. A soft, sensuous,
romantic fantasy. ISBN 1-56280-173-1   11.95

FORTY LOVE by Diana Simmonds. 288 pp. Joyous, heart-
warming romance. ISBN 1-56280-171-6   11.95

IN THE MOOD by Robbi Sommers. 160 pp. The queen of
erotic tension! ISBN 1-56280-172-4   11.95

SWIMMING CAT COVE by Lauren Douglas. 192 pp. 2nd
Allison O'Neil Mystery. ISBN 1-56280-168-6   11.95

THE LOVING LESBIAN by Claire McNab and Sharon Gedan.
240 pp. Explore the experiences that make lesbian love unique.
ISBN 1-56280-169-4   14.95

COURTED by Celia Cohen. 160 pp. Sparkling romantic
encounter. ISBN 1-56280-166-X   11.95

SEASONS OF THE HEART by Jackie Calhoun. 240 pp. Romance
through the years. ISBN 1-56280-167-8   11.95

K. C. BOMBER by Janet McClellan. 208 pp. 1st Tru North
mystery. ISBN 1-56280-157-0   11.95

LAST RITES by Tracey Richardson. 192 pp. 1st Stevie Houston
mystery. ISBN 1-56280-164-3   11.95

EMBRACE IN MOTION by Karin Kallmaker. 256 pp. A whirlwind
love affair. ISBN 1-56280-165-1   11.95

HOT CHECK by Peggy J. Herring. 192 pp. Will workaholic Alice
fall for guitarist Ricky? ISBN 1-56280-163-5   11.95

OLD TIES by Saxon Bennett. 176 pp. Can Cleo surrender to a
passionate new love? ISBN 1-56280-159-7   11.95

LOVE ON THE LINE by Laura DeHart Young. 176 pp. Will Stef
win Kay's heart? ISBN 1-56280-162-7   11.95

DEVIL'S LEG CROSSING by Kaye Davis. 192 pp. 1st Maris
Middleton mystery. ISBN 1-56280-158-9   11.95

COSTA BRAVA by Marta Balletbo Coll. 144 pp. Read the book,
see the movie! ISBN 1-56280-153-8   11.95

MEETING MAGDALENE & OTHER STORIES by
Marilyn Freeman. 144 pp. Read the book, see the movie!
ISBN 1-56280-170-8   11.95

SECOND FIDDLE by Kate 208 pp. 2nd P.I. Cassidy James
mystery.   ISBN 1-56280-169-6   11.95

LAUREL by Isabel Miller. 128 pp. By the author of the beloved
Patience and Sarah.   ISBN 1-56280-146-5   10.95

LOVE OR MONEY by Jackie Calhoun. 240 pp. The romance of
real life.   ISBN 1-56280-147-3   10.95

SMOKE AND MIRRORS by Pat Welch. 224 pp. 5th Helen Black
Mystery.   ISBN 1-56280-143-0   10.95

DANCING IN THE DARK edited by Barbara Grier & Christine
Cassidy. 272 pp. Erotic love stories by Naiad Press authors.
                                            ISBN 1-56280-144-9   14.95

TIME AND TIME AGAIN by Catherine Ennis. 176 pp. Passionate
love affair.   ISBN 1-56280-145-7   10.95

PAXTON COURT by Diane Salvatore. 256 pp. Erotic and wickedly
funny contemporary tale about the business of learning to live
together.   ISBN 1-56280-114-7   10.95

INNER CIRCLE by Claire McNab. 208 pp. 8th Carol Ashton
Mystery.   ISBN 1-56280-135-X   11.95

LESBIAN SEX: AN ORAL HISTORY by Susan Johnson.
240 pp. Need we say more?   ISBN 1-56280-142-2   14.95

WILD THINGS by Karin Kallmaker. 240 pp. By the undisputed
mistress of lesbian romance.   ISBN 1-56280-139-2   11.95

THE GIRL NEXT DOOR by Mindy Kaplan. 208 pp. Just what
you d expect.   ISBN 1-56280-140-6   11.95

NOW AND THEN by Penny Hayes. 240 pp. Romance on the
westward journey.   ISBN 1-56280-121-X   11.95

HEART ON FIRE by Diana Simmonds. 176 pp. The romantic and
erotic rival of *Curious Wine.*   ISBN 1-56280-152-X   11.95

DEATH AT LAVENDER BAY by Lauren Wright Douglas. 208 pp.
1st Allison O'Neil Mystery.   ISBN 1-56280-085-X   11.95

YES I SAID YES I WILL by Judith McDaniel. 272 pp. Hot
romance by famous author.   ISBN 1-56280-138-4   11.95

FORBIDDEN FIRES by Margaret C. Anderson. Edited by Mathilda
Hills. 176 pp. Famous author's "unpublished" Lesbian romance.
                                            ISBN 1-56280-123-6   21.95

SIDE TRACKS by Teresa Stores. 160 pp. Gender-bending
Lesbians on the road.   ISBN 1-56280-122-8   10.95

HOODED MURDER by Annette Van Dyke. 176 pp. 1st Jessie
Batelle Mystery.   ISBN 1-56280-134-1   10.95

WILDWOOD FLOWERS by Julia Watts. 208 pp. Hilarious and
heart-warming tale of true love.   ISBN 1-56280-127-9   10.95

NEVER SAY NEVER by Linda Hill. 224 pp. Rule #1: Never get
involved with . . .   ISBN 1-56280-126-0   11.95

THE SEARCH by Melanie McAllester. 240 pp. Exciting top cop
Tenny Mendoza case.   ISBN 1-56280-150-3   10.95

THE WISH LIST by Saxon Bennett. 192 pp. Romance through
the years.   ISBN 1-56280-125-2   10.95

FIRST IMPRESSIONS by Kate 208 pp. 1st P.I. Cassidy
James mystery.   ISBN 1-56280-133-3   10.95

OUT OF THE NIGHT by Kris Bruyer. 192 pp. Spine-tingling
thriller.   ISBN 1-56280-120-1   10.95

NORTHERN BLUE by Tracey Richardson. 224 pp. Police recruits
Miki & Miranda — passion in the line of fire. ISBN 1-56280-118-X   10.95

LOVE'S HARVEST by Peggy J. Herring. 176 pp. by the author of
Once More With Feeling.   ISBN 1-56280-117-1   10.95

THE COLOR OF WINTER by Lisa Shapiro. 208 pp. Romantic
love beyond your wildest dreams.   ISBN 1-56280-116-3   10.95

FAMILY SECRETS by Laura DeHart Young. 208 pp. Enthralling
romance and suspense.   ISBN 1-56280-119-8   10.95

INLAND PASSAGE by Jane Rule. 288 pp. Tales exploring conven-
tional & unconventional relationships.   ISBN 0-930044-56-8   10.95

DOUBLE BLUFF by Claire McNab. 208 pp. 7th Carol Ashton
Mystery.   ISBN 1-56280-096-5   10.95

BAR GIRLS by Lauran Hoffman. 176 pp. See the movie, read
the book!   ISBN 1-56280-115-5   10.95

THE FIRST TIME EVER edited by Barbara Grier & Christine
Cassidy. 272 pp. Love stories by Naiad Press authors.
                                             ISBN 1-56280-086-8   14.95

MISS PETTIBONE AND MISS McGRAW by Brenda Weathers.
208 pp. A charming ghostly love story.   ISBN 1-56280-151-1   10.95

CHANGES by Jackie Calhoun. 208 pp. Involved romance and
relationships.   ISBN 1-56280-083-3   10.95

FAIR PLAY by Rose Beecham. 256 pp. An Amanda Valentine
Mystery.   ISBN 1-56280-081-7   10.95

PAYBACK by Celia Cohen. 176 pp. A gripping thriller of romance,
revenge and betrayal.   ISBN 1-56280-084-1   10.95

THE BEACH AFFAIR by Barbara Johnson. 224 pp. Sizzling
summer romance/mystery/intrigue.   ISBN 1-56280-090-6   10.95

GETTING THERE by Robbi Sommers. 192 pp. Nobody does it
like Robbi!   ISBN 1-56280-099-X   10.95

FINAL CUT by Lisa Haddock. 208 pp. 2nd Carmen Ramirez
Mystery.   ISBN 1-56280-088-4   10.95

FLASHPOINT by Katherine V. Forrest. 256 pp. A Lesbian
blockbuster! ISBN 1-56280-079-5 10.95

CLAIRE OF THE MOON by Nicole Conn. Audio Book —
Read by Marianne Hyatt. ISBN 1-56280-113-9 16.95

FOR LOVE AND FOR LIFE: INTIMATE PORTRAITS OF
LESBIAN COUPLES by Susan Johnson. 224 pp.
ISBN 1-56280-091-4 14.95

DEVOTION by Mindy Kaplan. 192 pp. See the movie — read
the book! ISBN 1-56280-093-0 10.95

SOMEONE TO WATCH by Jaye Maiman. 272 pp. 4th Robin
Miller Mystery. ISBN 1-56280-095-7 10.95

GREENER THAN GRASS by Jennifer Fulton. 208 pp. A young
woman — a stranger in her bed. ISBN 1-56280-092-2 10.95

TRAVELS WITH DIANA HUNTER by Regine Sands. Erotic
lesbian romp. Audio Book (2 cassettes) ISBN 1-56280-107-4 16.95

CABIN FEVER by Carol Schmidt. 256 pp. Sizzling suspense
and passion. ISBN 1-56280-089-1 10.95

THERE WILL BE NO GOODBYES by Laura DeHart Young. 192
pp. Romantic love, strength, and friendship. ISBN 1-56280-103-1 10.95

FAULTLINE by Sheila Ortiz Taylor. 144 pp. Joyous comic
lesbian novel. ISBN 1-56280-108-2 9.95

OPEN HOUSE by Pat Welch. 176 pp. 4th Helen Black Mystery.
ISBN 1-56280-102-3 10.95

ONCE MORE WITH FEELING by Peggy J. Herring. 240 pp.
Lighthearted, loving romantic adventure. ISBN 1-56280-089-2 11.95

FOREVER by Evelyn Kennedy. 224 pp. Passionate romance — love
overcoming all obstacles. ISBN 1-56280-094-9 10.95

WHISPERS by Kris Bruyer. 176 pp. Romantic ghost story.
ISBN 1-56280-082-5 10.95

NIGHT SONGS by Penny Mickelbury. 224 pp. 2nd Gianna
Maglione Mystery. ISBN 1-56280-097-3 10.95

GETTING TO THE POINT by Teresa Stores. 256 pp. Classic
southern Lesbian novel. ISBN 1-56280-100-7 10.95

PAINTED MOON by Karin Kallmaker. 224 pp. Delicious
Kallmaker romance. ISBN 1-56280-075-2 11.95

THE MYSTERIOUS NAIAD edited by Katherine V. Forrest &
Barbara Grier. 320 pp. Love stories by Naiad Press authors.
ISBN 1-56280-074-4 14.95

DAUGHTERS OF A CORAL DAWN by Katherine V. Forrest.
240 pp. Tenth Anniversay Edition. ISBN 1-56280-104-X 11.95

BODY GUARD by Claire McNab. 208 pp. 6th Carol Ashton
Mystery. ISBN 1-56280-073-6 11.95

CACTUS LOVE by Lee Lynch. 192 pp. Stories by the beloved
storyteller.   ISBN 1-56280-071-X   9.95

SECOND GUESS by Rose Beecham. 216 pp. An Amanda
Valentine Mystery.   ISBN 1-56280-069-8   9.95

A RAGE OF MAIDENS by Lauren Wright Douglas. 240 pp.
6th Caitlin Reece Mystery.   ISBN 1-56280-068-X   10.95

TRIPLE EXPOSURE by Jackie Calhoun. 224 pp. Romantic
drama involving many characters.   ISBN 1-56280-067-1   10.95

PERSONAL ADS by Robbi Sommers. 176 pp. Sizzling short
stories.   ISBN 1-56280-059-0   11.95

CROSSWORDS by Penny Sumner. 256 pp. 2nd Victoria Cross
Mystery.   ISBN 1-56280-064-7   9.95

SWEET CHERRY WINE by Carol Schmidt. 224 pp. A novel of
suspense.   ISBN 1-56280-063-9   9.95

CERTAIN SMILES by Dorothy Tell. 160 pp. Erotic short stories.
                                                ISBN 1-56280-066-3   9.95

EDITED OUT by Lisa Haddock. 224 pp. 1st Carmen Ramirez
Mystery.   ISBN 1-56280-077-9   9.95

WEDNESDAY NIGHTS by Camarin Grae. 288 pp. Sexy
adventure.   ISBN 1-56280-060-4   11.95

SMOKEY O by Celia Cohen. 176 pp. Relationships on the
playing field.   ISBN 1-56280-057-4   9.95

KATHLEEN O'DONALD by Penny Hayes. 256 pp. Rose and
Kathleen find each other and employment in 1909 NYC.
                                                ISBN 1-56280-070-1   9.95

STAYING HOME by Elisabeth Nonas. 256 pp. Molly and Alix
want a baby . . . or do they?   ISBN 1-56280-076-0   10.95

TRUE LOVE by Jennifer Fulton. 240 pp. Six lesbians searching
for love in all the "right" places.   ISBN 1-56280-035-3   11.95

KEEPING SECRETS by Penny Mickelbury. 208 pp. 1st Gianna
Maglione Mystery.   ISBN 1-56280-052-3   9.95

THE ROMANTIC NAIAD edited by Katherine V. Forrest &
Barbara Grier. 336 pp. Love stories by Naiad Press authors.
                                                ISBN 1-56280-054-X   14.95

UNDER MY SKIN by Jaye Maiman. 336 pp. 3rd Robin Miller
Mystery.   ISBN 1-56280-049-3.   11.95

CAR POOL by Karin Kallmaker. 272pp. Lesbians on wheels
and then some!   ISBN 1-56280-048-5   11.95

NOT TELLING MOTHER: STORIES FROM A LIFE by Diane
Salvatore. 176 pp. Her 3rd novel.   ISBN 1-56280-044-2   9.95

GOBLIN MARKET by Lauren Wright Douglas. 240pp. 5th Caitlin
Reece Mystery.   ISBN 1-56280-047-7   10.95

FRIENDS AND LOVERS by Jackie Calhoun. 224 pp. Midwestern Lesbian lives and loves. ISBN 1-56280-041-8   11.95

BEHIND CLOSED DOORS by Robbi Sommers. 192 pp. Hot, erotic short stories. ISBN 1-56280-039-6   11.95

CLAIRE OF THE MOON by Nicole Conn. 192 pp. See the movie — read the book! ISBN 1-56280-038-8   11.95

SILENT HEART by Claire McNab. 192 pp. Exotic Lesbian romance. ISBN 1-56280-036-1   11.95

THE SPY IN QUESTION by Amanda Kyle Williams. 256 pp. A Madison McGuire Mystery. ISBN 1-56280-037-X   9.95

SAVING GRACE by Jennifer Fulton. 240 pp. Adventure and romantic entanglement. ISBN 1-56280-051-5   11.95

CURIOUS WINE by Katherine V. Forrest. 176 pp. Tenth Anniversary Edition. The most popular contemporary Lesbian love story.
ISBN 1-56280-053-1   11.95
Audio Book (2 cassettes)   ISBN 1-56280-105-8   16.95

CHAUTAUQUA by Catherine Ennis. 192 pp. Exciting, romantic adventure. ISBN 1-56280-032-9   9.95

A PROPER BURIAL by Pat Welch. 192 pp. 3rd Helen Black Mystery. ISBN 1-56280-033-7   9.95

SILVERLAKE HEAT: A Novel of Suspense by Carol Schmidt. 240 pp. Rhonda is as hot as Laney's dreams. ISBN 1-56280-031-0   9.95

LOVE, ZENA BETH by Diane Salvatore. 224 pp. The most talked about lesbian novel of the nineties! ISBN 1-56280-030-2   10.95

A DOORYARD FULL OF FLOWERS by Isabel Miller. 160 pp. Stories incl. 2 sequels to *Patience and Sarah.* ISBN 1-56280-029-9   9.95

MURDER BY TRADITION by Katherine V. Forrest. 288 pp. 4th Kate Delafield Mystery. ISBN 1-56280-002-7   11.95

THE EROTIC NAIAD edited by Katherine V. Forrest & Barbara Grier. 224 pp. Love stories by Naiad Press authors.
ISBN 1-56280-026-4   14.95

DEAD CERTAIN by Claire McNab. 224 pp. 5th Carol Ashton Mystery. ISBN 1-56280-027-2   9.95

CRAZY FOR LOVING by Jaye Maiman. 320 pp. 2nd Robin Miller Mystery. ISBN 1-56280-025-6   11.95

UNCERTAIN COMPANIONS by Robbi Sommers. 204 pp. Steamy, erotic novel. ISBN 1-56280-017-5   11.95

A TIGER'S HEART by Lauren W. Douglas. 240 pp. 4th Caitlin Reece Mystery. ISBN 1-56280-018-3   9.95

PAPERBACK ROMANCE by Karin Kallmaker. 256 pp. A delicious romance. ISBN 1-56280-019-1   10.95

I LEFT MY HEART by Jaye Maiman. 320 pp. 1st Robin Miller
Mystery.   ISBN 0-941483-72-X   11.95

THE PRICE OF SALT by Patricia Highsmith (writing as Claire
Morgan). 288 pp. Classic lesbian novel, first issued in 1952 . . .
acknowledged by its author under her own, very famous, name.
                                      ISBN 1-56280-003-5   11.95

SIDE BY SIDE by Isabel Miller. 256 pp. From beloved author of
Patience and Sarah.   ISBN 0-941483-77-0   10.95

STAYING POWER: LONG TERM LESBIAN COUPLES by
Susan E. Johnson. 352 pp. Joys of coupledom. ISBN 0-941-483-75-4   14.95

SLICK by Camarin Grae. 304 pp. Exotic, erotic adventure.
                                      ISBN 0-941483-74-6   9.95

NINTH LIFE by Lauren Wright Douglas. 256 pp. 2nd Caitlin
Reece Mystery.   ISBN 0-941483-50-9   9.95

PLAYERS by Robbi Sommers. 192 pp. Sizzling, erotic novel.
                                      ISBN 0-941483-73-8   9.95

MURDER AT RED ROOK RANCH by Dorothy Tell. 224 pp.
1st Poppy Dillworth Mystery.   ISBN 0-941483-80-0   8.95

A ROOM FULL OF WOMEN by Elisabeth Nonas. 256 pp.
Contemporary Lesbian lives.   ISBN 0-941483-69-X   9.95

THEME FOR DIVERSE INSTRUMENTS by Jane Rule. 208 pp.
Powerful romantic lesbian stories.   ISBN 0-941483-63-0   8.95

CLUB 12 by Amanda Kyle Williams. 288 pp. Espionage thriller
featuring a lesbian agent!   ISBN 0-941483-64-9   9.95

DEATH DOWN UNDER by Claire McNab. 240 pp. 3rd Carol
Ashton Mystery.   ISBN 0-941483-39-8   10.95

MONTANA FEATHERS by Penny Hayes. 256 pp. Vivian and
Elizabeth find love in frontier Montana.   ISBN 0-941483-61-4   9.95

LIFESTYLES by Jackie Calhoun. 224 pp. Contemporary Lesbian
lives and loves.   ISBN 0-941483-57-6   10.95

MURDER BY THE BOOK by Pat Welch. 256 pp. 1st Helen
Black Mystery.   ISBN 0-941483-59-2   9.95

THERE'S SOMETHING I'VE BEEN MEANING TO TELL YOU
Ed. by Loralee MacPike. 288 pp. Gay men and lesbians coming out
to their children.   ISBN 0-941483-44-4   9.95

These are just a few of the many Naiad Press titles — we are the oldest and
largest lesbian/feminist publishing company in the world. We also offer an
enormous selection of lesbian video products. Please request a complete
catalog. We offer personal service; we encourage and welcome direct mail
orders from individuals who have limited access to bookstores carrying our
publications.